There was
no turning back now...

She'd tried to stay away from him, but he was everything she had ever wanted and more than she'd imagined. The sudden realization sent a tremor through her.

"Don't be afraid of me," Matt whispered huskily as he felt her tremble in his arms.

"I'm not," Lauren admitted in a small voice. "I'm afraid of me—afraid of everything that's happened. It's all too quick and fast."

"That's the way love is," he said softly. "There's nothing very practical or organized about it."

He bent his head, and the possessive need of his kiss thrilled her. It was true, she thought as a river of happiness ran through her. She did love him. She had denied it to herself for days...for weeks, but there was no denying it any longer. She loved him and wanted him, and nothing could come between them, she thought fiercely. Nothing!

SANDRA MARTON lives on Long Island, not far from the glitter of Manhattan and the lovely stretches of beach bordering the Atlantic. Her husband likes to tell people he's the inspiration for her romance book heroes. Sandra used to laugh at that, until she realized that all her heroes are tall, dark and usually blue-eyed—the perfect description of her husband. They have two children, a dog and three cats—altogether a big happy family.

Books by Sandra Marton

HARLEQUIN PRESENTS
988—A GAME OF DECEIT

SANDRA MARTON

out of the shadows

Harlequin Books

TORONTO • NEW YORK • LONDON
AMSTERDAM • PARIS • SYDNEY • HAMBURG
STOCKHOLM • ATHENS • TOKYO • MILAN

To my husband: With love, gratitude,
and, most of all—GOTCHA!

Harlequin Presents first edition November 1987
ISBN 0-373-11027-8

Original hardcover edition published in 1986
by Mills & Boon Limited

PROLOGUE

WINTER had come to the coast of northern California. The grey, sunless sky and the low clouds sweeping menacingly from the west promised nothing, but more of the chilling rain that had ceased only minutes earlier. On a low Pacific hillside, dwarfed by the flat, metallic sky, two people stood beside the ochre-coloured earth of a newly opened grave.

Lauren Webster raised her head as the minister ended his final prayer. A flurry of wind, bearing the salt tang of the ocean, blew across the grave and she shivered and turned towards the man beside her.

'Thank you for everything, Reverend Dodd,' she said in a clear, low-pitched voice. 'I know my mother would have been pleased. It was just the kind of service she'd have wanted.'

The minister smiled and shrugged his shoulders. 'I hope so. I didn't know your mother very well, Ms Webster. I only visited her once after her car accident.'

'I'm sure you were a comfort, Reverend Dodd. I wish she'd let them notify me right away.'

The minister turned his collar up against the wind. 'She didn't want to worry you. She said you had a lot to do, that you'd just moved to New York City.'

Lauren nodded in agreement. 'Just a few months ago. My company transferred me.'

'Yes, so your mother said. She was very proud of you, Ms Webster.'

A faint smile touched her face. 'Not always, Reverend Dodd.'

A car door slammed, the sound echoing eerily among the marble headstones. Startled, Lauren turned and looked towards the road. A tall, broad-shouldered figure was striding rapidly up the hill, his hands jammed into the pockets of his raincoat. The breath caught in her throat as the man reached the crest of the hill and paused.

'. . . Stop in and visit before you leave San Jacinto, Ms Webster.'

Mutely, she nodded her head, only barely aware of the minister's polite comments. The wind gusted again, sighing through the small cemetery, scattering dark, brittle leaves in its path. Lauren shivered and took a hesitant step forward, her eyes locked on the man.

The Reverend Mr Dodd looked from Lauren to the figure on the hillside. 'That's Matthew Chandler,' he said. 'Do you know him?'

'I . . . yes, I know him,' she murmured, dropping her glance to the damp earth piled at her feet.

She sensed him walking slowly towards her, until finally they were only feet apart. Wasn't it incredible? she thought . . . After all this time, even though she knew he was married, her heart was pounding. She raised her head until at last their eyes met. His showed nothing of what he might be feeling, and she could only hope hers concealed the hurt, the longing . . . She wasn't sure what she felt for this man, this intimate stranger who stood opposite her. She knew only that it required great effort to hold her ground.

'It's good to see you, Matt . . .'

He smiled and her heart seemed to turn over. 'It's good to see you, too,' he said quietly.

The simple words, spoken softly across the raw earth, achieved what the funeral service had not.

Tears welled in Lauren Webster's eyes and at last she began to weep.

CHAPTER ONE

LAUREN WEBSTER leaned forward and peered near-sightedly at her reflection in the mirror. Frowning with concentration, she tugged at a stray lock of sun-streaked blonde hair and smoothed it carefully away from her face. Although it was early evening, the heat of the July day hadn't lessened and her long, thick hair was behaving as it always did during the hot California summers, resisting all attempts to be tamed.

She turned and glanced into the mirror again as she smoothed down the skirt of her white silk dress. The mass of wheaten hair brushed up to the top of her head and secured there with an ivory comb suited the sophistication of the dress far better than the usual spill of loose curls down her back. Still, the young woman in the mirror was a stranger, a chic, cool-looking parody of herself.

With a sigh, Lauren turned away from the mirror. Through the thin wall separating her small bedroom from her mother's, she could hear the older woman's footsteps hurrying back and forth as she dressed. It was too late to try and change her mother's mind about the dress. Besides, she'd only start an argument she'd lost once already, when, with a triumphant flourish, her mother had draped the silk dress across Lauren's bed and announced that she was to wear it to the San Jacinto Country Club dance that night.

'It's beautiful,' Lauren had admitted slowly,

10

touching a finger to the luxurious fabric, 'but it's not really me. I was going to wear my green chiffon . . .'

'That's precisely what I was afraid of,' her mother had said crisply, as she bent and rummaged through the shoes lined up on the bottom shelf of the closet. 'A dress you wore to your senior prom four years ago is hardly suitable for tonight. Didn't they teach you the importance of dressing properly in business school?' She clucked her tongue in annoyance and looked up. 'What did you do with those white sandals? Don't tell me I'm going to have to go out and buy a pair at this hour!'

Lauren sighed and reached into the back of the closet. 'Here they are, Mother. But I won't need them if I wear the green dress. It's not that this one isn't lovely,' she added quickly, before the older woman could say anything, 'it's just that I'd feel more comfortable in something of my own.'

There was a rasp of irritation in her mother's voice. 'This is your own, Lauren. I bought it for you the other day, after Mrs Harrow asked us to join her at the Club this evening.'

'She asked us? Come on, Mother—you didn't give her much choice! Telling her how much I wanted to attend, how much I wanted to renew old friendships now that I've come back from San Francisco. What 'old friendships', Mother? I was never part of that Country Club bunch.'

'Nonsense! You grew up here—you know those people, Lauren. And it's time you were part of them.'

'And you told her I'm going to be a management trainee at Chandler Vineyards. What will she think when she finds out I'm in the secretarial pool?'

'She won't find out, unless you tell her and make a liar out of me. Besides, trainees have to start some place, don't they? Once your supervisor gets to know you, I'm sure you'll be promoted. And I'll put in a good word for you; I've worked at Chandler for so long that I know all the right people . . .'

'I don't want you to pull strings for me, Mother. I told you that.'

Mrs Webster sighed and plucked a piece of thread from the white silk dress. 'Let's not quarrel tonight, please.' She smiled and touched her hand to Lauren's cheek. 'You know how proud I am of you, baby,' she said softly. 'You're all I have in this whole world. I just want you to have a good life. Is that so awful?'

The words were so familiar, Lauren thought, looking at her mother's hopeful smile. How could you argue with someone who had sacrificed everything for you?

'No, I guess not,' she said slowly. 'I know you want the best for me . . .'

'Only the best, Lauren. You know that. It's bad enough that you had to work for two years so we could afford to send you to business school . . .'

'I didn't mind,' Lauren said quickly.

'No, but I did.' The older woman took her daughter's hands in hers. 'I want you to have all the things you'd have had if your father had lived, things people like the Harrows take for granted. Good clothes, the right friends . . . You'll love the dance at the Club tonight, baby. Everybody talks about their July the Fourth firework display, and the tables are all done in red, white and blue. That's why I bought you that white dress, Lauren.' She smiled winsomely and sighed. 'I guess I'm a terrible mother, hmm? Buying you nice clothes, worrying about your future, getting you a chance to go to the July the Fourth dance . . .' Her smile broadened as Lauren's lips began to curl upward. 'How can you stand living with such an awful mother?'

'Okay,' Lauren sighed, giving in to the inevitable. 'I'll wear the dress. And I won't mention the secretarial pool.'

Her mother patted her cheek. 'Good girl,' she said briskly. 'And Lauren, for heaven's sake, do something with that mane of hair!'

Well, it had taken an hour, but she'd done something with it, Lauren thought unhappily, although the mass of blonde curls looked as if the slightest breeze would send it tumbling. In fact, wasn't the comb loosening already? She leaned towards the mirror and then fumbled for her glasses in the handbag lying on the dresser.

'I don't believe it,' her mother said harshly.

Lauren gasped and whirled around. 'You startled me, Mother! I didn't hear you open the door.'

'I startled you? I think the shoe's on the other foot, isn't it? Surely you aren't serious, Lauren. Why are you wearing your glasses?'

'So I can see, Mother,' she answered patiently. 'My hair's falling down, and I'd like to know if my lipstick is on straight.'

'Stop exaggerating, for goodness' sake. You're not that nearsighted. If only the contact lenses we ordered were ready . . . You simply can't wear glasses tonight, they'll spoil the way you look in that dress.'

'So will falling down the stairs at the Club, if I can't see them,' Lauren said mildly. 'Have you thought of that?'

'Don't be ridiculous! That's what banisters are for. Besides, I'll be with you.' Her mother's voice softened and she smiled. 'And once we're there, there'll be plenty of young men happy to take you by the hand and escort you safely to the dance floor. You look beautiful, Lauren. I knew that white silk was made for you the minute I saw it. Now come along, child. I promised Mrs Harrow we'd meet them at eight. Late entrances are all right for the *haut monde*, but we'd better be on time.'

In fact, Lauren thought a short while later, the Harrows probably would have preferred that they make no appearance at all. Her mother greeted them effusively, but Mrs Harrow's smile seemed forced and her husband only nodded as he rose from his chair. There were two other couples at the table. The women barely smiled, but Lauren was uncomfortably aware of the sly, appraising glances of their husbands.

She sat stiffly through the first course, picking at her shrimp cocktail, wishing she had not given in to her mother's pleas that they attend the dance. The band was playing, but the music wasn't loud enough to keep her from hearing what her mother was saying. She was forcing her way into a conversation that seemed determined to exclude her, centring as it did on last winter's trips to the South of France and the Caribbean. The talk turned to the difficulty of finding dependable household servants, and Lauren winced inwardly at the bright, artificial sound of her mother's voice as she described how impossible it was to hire a reliable housekeeper.

Stop it! she thought fiercely, bending her head to hide the angry, embarrassed blush she felt spilling across her face. They know you can't afford a maid, Mother. You're not kidding anybody. Why do you do this?

She glanced up and caught the two strange women staring at her mother. Even without her glasses, she could see that one had a look of pity on her face and the other wore a faint, amused smile. A mixture of sorrow and anger welled up inside her and her fork dropped from seemingly numb fingers and fell to the floor. Her mother's head rose sharply at the clattering sound. She frowned disapprovingly and then her face resumed its bland, interested lines as she turned back to Mrs Harrow. With a faint shudder Lauren leaned down to retrieve the fork.

The man next to her bent quickly and his hand encircled her wrist. 'Don't bother,' he said pleasantly. 'We'll get you another.' A smile lit his florid, beefy face. 'How is it we've never seen you here before?' he asked quietly, his fingers still clamped firmly to her wrist.

Lauren smiled politely. 'I was at the Club's Midsummer dance several years ago,' she said, trying unsuccessfully to free her hand from his.

'Really? I must have missed that one. Certainly, if I'd been there, I wouldn't have forgotten such a beautiful young woman.' His fingers began to stroke the inside of her wrist. 'I understand you've only just come back to San Jacinto, and you want to meet all the right people.'

'I already know all the right people,' she said quickly, wondering how he could continue to keep such a pleasant, innocent look on his face while his sweaty hand gave hers quite a different message.

'Your mother doesn't seem to think so. I get the impression she wants you to make some contacts here tonight, and I'd be happy to be one of them.'

Lauren smiled sweetly. 'And I get the impression your wife would be quite upset if I told her what you're up to. If you don't let go of me this second, that's just what I'm going to do.'

His face whitened and his hand dropped from hers. Biting back her anger, Lauren pushed back her chair and got to her feet.

'Excuse me,' she said quietly, deliberately ignoring her mother's puzzled frown. 'I . . . I'll be back in a few minutes.'

It would take at least that long to calm down and get control of herself, she thought, hurrying past the few couples gliding across the polished dance floor, hoping that the blurred white rectangle she could barely see on the far wall was the door to the ladies' room.

Nothing had changed, she thought angrily. Her mother was still bent on clawing her way into San Jacinto's social register, and it was still just as determined to keep her out. The last time she'd been in this place, she'd been eighteen years old, a naïve Cinderella looking for her Prince Charming, until she'd discovered that there was nothing magical about the young men who had clustered around her that night. They'd seen her as an oddity, an attractive object to toy with for the evening and, with a bit of luck, other evenings to come, but not a girl to take on a date or introduce to their friends. The man back at the table might be older, but he was no different. Just wait until the evening was over! she thought furiously. She'd tell her mother what 'the right people' were really like. She'd tell her . . .

'Whoops! I'm terribly sorry, I'm afraid I didn't see you coming.'

Lauren gasped as a cold liquid splashed against her and trickled down the front of her dress. She looked up at the man standing before her and shook her head with embarrassment.

'It wasn't your fault,' she said quickly. 'I wasn't

looking where I was going.' The man smiled—she could tell that much, although his features were somewhat blurred—and held something out to her.

'Here,' he said in a low, pleasant voice, 'you'd better use that to blot up the champagne. You wouldn't want to spoil such a lovely dress.'

She nodded and snatched at the table napkin in his hand. 'Thank you,' she murmured, dabbing at her dress. 'It'll be fine.' Hurriedly, she moved past him and pushed open the door she'd been heading towards. She squinted at the sign on it, but the letters were a wavering blur.

'Hey—wait a minute! Why are you going in there?'

Lauren's face pinkened as his voice called after her. What kind of stupid question was that? Why did he think someone went into the ladies' room . . .? The door slammed shut, and she blinked in surprise. The room she'd entered was pitch black. She turned quickly and rattled the doorknob, but the door had locked behind her. Slowly, she felt her way along the wall, feeling for a light switch, but her hand touched nothing but the coolness of bare brick. The room felt small, although she couldn't be certain, and it smelled musty and unused.

'Damn!' she muttered. 'Well, I guess it isn't the ladies' room.'

The door opened just long enough to admit a slash of light from the ballroom and a blare of music.

'No,' a voice said mildly, 'it isn't the ladies' room.'

Lauren drew in her breath as she recognised the voice. It was the man she'd bumped into on the dance floor. She turned towards where she knew he must be standing and cleared her throat.

'Is there a light switch in here, do you know?' she

asked in a tone she hoped sounded casual and unconcerned. 'I haven't been able to find one.'

'Of course you haven't,' he said mildly. 'That's because there isn't any. There's a pull chain, however,' he added, and in a second, the room was flooded with light.

Lauren blinked and glanced around her. She was in what seemed to be a small storeroom. Folding chairs and boxes were stacked to one side, and several cartons lay against the back wall. Her rescuer was lounging against the wall next to her, close enough so that she could see him more clearly this time. He was tall and good-looking, and his dark blue eyes were narrowed with amusement.

'Well, thank you again,' she said stiffly. 'I guess they've moved the ladies' room.'

She cringed as the foolish remark left her mouth, but the man only nodded solemnly.

'Seems so,' he agreed. 'Although it was right where it was supposed to be when I passed it half an hour ago.'

'Look,' she said, taking a deep breath 'I know this all seems very funny to you, but I'm finding it a bit difficult to laugh. So if you'll just step aside and get out of my way, I'll be leaving.'

He nodded and gestured at the door. 'By all means. Don't let me stop you.'

Lauren slipped past him and tugged uselessly at the doorknob. After a few seconds, she bit her lip.

'It's locked,' she said helplessly.

He sighed and shrugged his shoulders. 'Yes, it tends to do that. There's a little sign there—by the knob. Just follow the directions and the door will open.'

She peered intently at the tiny white marks to

which he pointed. They were letters, all right, but they might as well have been in Chinese. It was impossible for her to read them. Uncomfortably aware of the stranger's scrutiny and the smile on his face, she fumbled unsuccessfully at the knob again.

'Er—look,' she said finally, feeling like an absolute fool, 'I never was very good at directions. If you could just open this door . . .'

'My pleasure,' he said smoothly. 'Directions like those can be hard to follow, can't they? Complicated ones, I mean.' He came around behind her, and she felt his body lean slightly against hers. Involuntarily, she stiffened and tried to move away from him, but there was nowhere to go. She felt the warmth of his breath against her neck as he reached around her. 'These are particularly difficult,' he added. 'They say: "Door locks automatically. Depress latch to open".'

Lauren winced with embarrassment as the lock clicked open. The man chuckled softly as she flung open the door and almost ran from the room. She'd been at the San Jacinto Country Club for less than an hour, and already she'd been twice reminded that she didn't belong there, she thought grimly. Well, enough was enough. Her mother could spend the rest of the evening providing amusement for San Jacinto's upper crust; she was retiring from the game. Surely there would be no one on the terrace overlooking the lake, at least not while dinner was still being served. It was the perfect spot to hide for a hour or so and then find her mother and plead a headache or illness or whatever it took to get away from this place and the people in it.

She dodged among the couples on the dance floor, hoping they would shield her from her mother's eyes,

and headed for the french windows at the rear of the
ballroom. Breathing a sigh of relief, she started down
the broad marble steps that led to the terrace.

'There are three steps,' an all-too-familiar voice
murmured in her ear as a hand grasped her elbow
and almost lifted her off her feet. 'Be careful you
don't trip.'

'Now, that's enough,' she said angrily. 'Really, I'm
perfectly capable of walking downstairs by myself!'

He laughed and his hold on her tightened. 'I'm
sure you are, but only if you can see them. Now, now,
now,' he said soothingly when she tried to pull free,
'don't fight me. I'm just going to deposit you
somewhere safe. Here we are,' he said at last.
'There's a bench here, can you see it? Just sit down—
that's it—and you'll be fine. The lake is just over that
way.'

With a final wrench, Lauren pulled free of his
hand. 'For God's sake,' she shrilled, 'I'm not an
idiot! And I'm not blind. What do you take me for?'

'An extremely nearsighted young woman. Don't
you have a pair of glasses?'

'Of course I have,' she snapped, 'not that it's any
of your business.'

He sat down next to her and grinned. 'Then why
on earth aren't you wearing them?'

It was such a logical question, and he asked it so
matter-of-factly that suddenly all the fight went out
of her.

'I left them in the car,' she admitted quietly.
'Wasn't that dumb?'

'I'm glad you did. Otherwise, I wouldn't have had
to come to your rescue, and we'd never have met.' He
paused and smiled at her. 'Although I'm sure I'd
have noticed the most beautiful woman in the room,

sooner or later.'

A faint blush spread over Lauren's cheeks. 'Look,' she said nervously, 'you don't have to stay out here with me. The lake is big enough so I can't possibly mistake it for a puddle, and I promise I'll ask someone to take me by the hand and lead me inside when it's time to leave.'

'You mean you're going to stay out here all evening?' She nodded her head and he looked at her enquiringly. 'What's the matter?' he asked lightly. 'Don't you like the food? I can't say I blame you; if that shrimp cocktail was any example of what the rest of the meal is going to be like, I think I might pass on it, too. I'd heard the San Jacinto Country Club had the best kitchen in town. Guess I heard wrong.'

Lauren looked at him with renewed interest. 'You mean you aren't a member either?'

'Nope, just a guest. Well, so you *can* smile,' he said teasingly. 'I was beginning to wonder. Did I finally say the right thing?'

She blushed. 'It's just that I thought you . . . I had a run-in with one of the members before, you see, and . . .' She raised her chin and looked the stranger straight in the eye. 'I don't like this place very much,' she finished defiantly.

He smiled again, and she found herself wishing she had her glasses on so she could see if he was really as handsome as he seemed.

'It's not my favourite place either. Still, I'm glad I came tonight.'

There was no mistaking the meaning of his words, and her blush deepened.

'Did you come with a——Who did you come with?' she asked, before she could censor her own thoughts.

'I was just about to ask you the same question,' he laughed. 'No, I'm not here with a date. I'm here, under protest, with my father.'

The directness of his answer pleased her, and a smile danced at the corners of her mouth. 'That makes two of us, except I lodged my protest with my mother. She wouldn't take no for an answer, either.'

The man smiled. 'Well, I'm glad we both listened to our elders this once!' He got to his feet and held his hand out to her. 'The food here may leave something to be desired, but the band is pretty good. It would be a pity to waste the music. Would you like to dance?'

For the first time since they'd come outside, Lauren became aware of the soft swell of music drifting from the open french windows. Surely it wouldn't hurt to dance with him for a few minutes? At least she could show him she wasn't completely incompetent. She smiled and placed her hand in his.

'Yes,' she said pleasantly, 'I'd love to.'

He drew her into his arms and they began to move slowly across the flagstoned terrace, away from the doors leading to the ballroom. Even though she was wearing high-heeled sandals, she felt small next to him. His body felt lean and hard against hers, and she could feel the tautness of muscle under her hand where it lay on his shoulder. As the band followed one dreamy old standard with another, he drew her closer against him until finally she laid her head under his chin and closed her eyes.

The still night air was faintly scented with honeysuckle, just as it had been on the night, four years before, when she'd last been at the Club. She remembered how eagerly she had looked forward to that dance, and how angry and upset she'd been when she had overheard two of the boys she had danced with discussing her as if she were a prize to win in a lottery. She glanced up at the stranger from beneath her lashes. He was certainly not a boy, she thought, closing her eyes again and blushing as she felt the hard outlines of his body against hers. And he hadn't been here that night; she'd have noticed if he had. He was a guest, not a member, he'd said ... Still, she knew nothing about him, nothing except how handsome he seemed, how charming he was, how content she felt in his arms. She didn't even know his name ...

'What's your name?' he whispered suddenly.

It's as if he read my mind, she thought, smiling and lifting her head. 'Lauren,' she said. 'What's yours?'

'Matt,' he answered, his hand lifting from the small of her back and bringing her head against his chest again.

She felt a momentary confusion at how willingly she settled back into his arms.

'Won't your father be looking for you?'

He chuckled softly. 'Won't your mother be looking for you?'

They were laughing quietly, joined in their shared conspiracy, when the music stopped with a soft wail of trumpets. Matt's arm slipped to her waist.

'Look,' he said, 'the moon's risen.'

Lauren followed his gaze across the still, dark water of the lake to where the sky was just changing from the dark indigo of sunset to the blackness of night.

' "Moon of the purple and silent west," ' she whispered, and Matt's arm tightened around her.

' "Remember me one of your lovers of dreams," '

he finished. She stared at him in surprise, and he smiled. 'Carl Sandburg's one of my favourite poets, too, although there's another poem of his that suits this night better.' He drew her closer to him. ' "Listen a while," ' he murmured. ' "The moon is a lovely woman . . ." '

His breath was warm against her ear, and she felt flushed and confused. Suddenly there was a deep roar from the other side of the lake and a cascade of orange chrysanthemums seemed to explode in the sky.

'Oh, Matt, the fireworks have started . . .'

'I noticed,' he said softly.

Lauren glanced at his face. He was staring at her, not at the coloured lights streaming towards them. There was a burst of white light in the night sky and a shower of blue flowers arced downward.

'You're not watching the fireworks,' she said faintly. 'And they're so lovely . . .'

In the light of the exploding fireworks, his face was a shadowed series of planes and angles. His eyes seemed so dark, she thought suddenly, almost as dark and mysterious as the night sky. She trembled as he turned towards her and put his other arm around her.

'Lovely,' he agreed in a whisper. 'The loveliest I've ever seen.'

But it was not the fireworks he was talking about. Lauren knew that, as surely as she knew he was going to kiss her.

She closed her eyes as he bent his head towards her. It was all like a dream, she thought, as his lips touched hers in a gentle, tentative kiss. This handsome stranger, the moonlit night, the brilliant lights exploding in the sky . . . Her heartbeat quickened as his hands tightened on her back and drew her closer to him, his mouth still on hers. Her lips parted under the increasing demand of his, and she wound her arms around his neck, lost in the wonder of the feelings he had aroused in her.

'Lauren . . .' he whispered, 'Lauren . . .'

'Lauren!'

She gasped and wrenched herself free of Matt's embrace as her mother's voice cut through the night like an exploding rocket. The older woman was standing a few feet away, but even without her glasses Lauren could see the pinched, angry look on her face.

'We're leaving now, Lauren,' she said with clipped precision. 'Come along.'

Lauren looked from Matt to her mother. 'Mother,' she said haltingly, 'I'd like you to meet Matt . . .' She paused, aware for the first time that she didn't even know this man's last name. To her surprise, he was walking towards her mother, his right hand outstretched.

'Good evening, Mrs Webster,' he said pleasantly. 'It's nice to see you away from the office.'

'Mr Chandler,' she acknowledged frostily, barely touching her hand to his. She turned away and motioned to Lauren. 'Our car is being brought around to the front, Lauren. Hurry, please.'

Lauren looked at Matt Chandler in bewilderment. 'Matt Chandler?' she said slowly. 'Matthew Chandler? Is that who you are?'

'Yes,' he said quickly, turning towards her. 'Does it matter?'

The colour rose to her cheeks. 'You said . . . you said you weren't a member of the Club . . . you said you were a guest . . .'

'I am, Lauren. My father is a member.'

'Lauren! You've kept me waiting long enough. Do you have any idea how humiliating it's been, sitting at that table, wondering where you'd disappeared to?'

Lauren hurried to her mother's side. 'I'm sorry,' she said 'But those people . . .'

'Stop arguing with me!' hissed Mrs Webster, her fingers biting into Lauren's arm as she hurried her from the terrace. 'Haven't you done enough? First you simply walked off and left me, and then I find you here with . . . with a man like that!' She grasped her daughter's arm more firmly and began to hurry her along the side of the building. 'At least you had the decency to move away from the doors before you made a spectacle of yourself. There are people there watching the fireworks. Suppose someone saw you?'

'Lauren . . . wait!' Unthinkingly, Lauren slowed at the sound of Matt's voice and she glanced over her shoulder. 'I'll call you,' he said, but she didn't need the pressure of her mother's hand to make her shake her head.

'Don't bother,' she said stiffly. 'Just go back to your friends inside and have a good time.'

'Lauren . . .'

The two women hurried along the narrow pathway skirting the clubhouse until they reached the front. With a sigh of relief, Lauren slid behind the wheel of her old Ford and snatched up her glasses from the dashboard. Angrily, she stepped down hard on the accelerator as soon as her mother had settled in beside her.

'Slow down, if you please!' the older woman snapped. 'Don't add a speeding ticket or an accident to everything else you've done tonight. I spent days making up to that snooty Helen Harrow just to get us this invitation, and two weeks' pay on that dress you're wearing, and you repay me by making a fool of me in front of everybody! It was a wasted evening, Lauren. All the fine young men I wanted you to meet . . .'

Lauren slowed the car and glanced over at her mother. 'I didn't want to come in the first place, remember? And I certainly didn't want this dress. As for the "fine young men" you wanted me to meet,' she added with bitter sarcasm, 'if you'd paid any attention to what I've been telling you the past few years, you'd have known what they think of someone like me. They date and marry their own kind, Mother. Girls like me are good for only one thing, as far as they're concerned.'

'That's a fine speech, coming from someone who just did God knows what with Matthew Chandler!'

'I didn't do anything I'm ashamed of,' Lauren answered quickly, grateful that the darkness hid her flaming cheeks. 'Believe me, if I'd known he was one of them, I'd never even have spoken to him. But I'm surprised you're so annoyed, Mother. Isn't Matthew Chandler one of the "fine young men" you're so eager to have me meet?'

Evelyn Webster snorted softly. 'Why are you twisting my words? There are young men from fine families . . .'

'That means from wealthy families, doesn't it, Mother?'

'Matthew Chandler,' Evelyn said with disdain, ignoring her daughter's comment, 'isn't the sort who marries anybody. I could tell you stories about him— anyone who works at Chandler Vineyards could. The man is no good.' Her voice softened and she reached out and touched Lauren's hand. 'Why won't you let me help you make a good life for yourself? I know the people here; I can introduce you to the ones it pays to know; I can . . .'

Lauren pulled the car into the driveway of their small house and switched off the ignition. 'Listen to me, Mother,' she said, her voice tense with barely controlled anger. 'I was going to stay in San Francisco and find a job after I finished school. I only came home because you begged me to.'

'Lauren . . .'

'I owe you a great deal, Mother. I know how much you've sacrificed for me over the years so that I could have nice clothes and take tennis lessons and go to business school, but you must start letting me live my own life.' She turned towards her mother and took both her hands in hers. 'I love you, Mom,' she said evenly, 'but I want you to stop interfering in my life.'

'But a man like Matthew Chandler——'

'I'm not talking about Matthew Chandler,' said Lauren, irritation creeping into her voice. 'I despise the Matthew Chandlers of this world, don't you understand? I don't know why people like that are so important to you, but I hate the way they've made you beg for crumbs. I hate the way they treat you. I . . .' She took a trembling breath and started again. 'Don't worry about Matthew Chandler,' she said calmly. 'I don't ever intend to see him again.'

'Good. He's not what I want for you. But there are others——'

'Mother!' Lauren's voice was sharp with anger and frustration. 'If you want me to stay in San Jacinto, you have to stop trying to arrange my life for me. Do you understand?'

There was a lengthy silence, broken only by the

faint chirping and whirring sounds of the summer
night. Finally, Mrs Webster sighed.

'Of course I want you to stay, Lauren. You're all I
have.'

'Then you'll stop interfering in my life?'

The pause this time was briefer. 'I'll always do
what's best for you, Lauren. You know that.'

It was not until months later that Lauren realised
how cryptic an answer that had been.

CHAPTER TWO

THE vine-covered fieldstone building that housed Chandler Vineyards stood at the top of a low hill overlooking the Napa Valley, surrounded by fields of carefully tended grapes. Lauren's desk was one of several in a large first-floor office. Her job seemed easy compared to the demanding rigidity of her business school teachers. So far, even her weakest skill—taking dictation—had been more than adequate for the work she had been assigned. In fact, after almost two weeks, she'd begun to feel slightly bored with the monotony of her daily routine.

At first, half expecting Matthew Chandler to seek her out, she had been apprehensive and nervous. Certainly, as Vice-President of the winery, he could find her easily enough if he wanted to. As the days went by without a glimpse of him, she found herself beginning to wonder why he hadn't looked for her. It wasn't as if she wanted to see him again, she told herself. Still, if she did, she would have the chance to vindicate herself. The man had been toying with her that night, hadn't he? He'd been making a fool of her until her mother spoiled things for him. Everything he'd said and done had been part of a farce . . . She was entitled to tell him what she thought of him and his kind. She hadn't said half the things she should have before her mother rushed her away.

At least her worries about her mother's interference at work had been groundless. Evelyn Webster, working down the hall in the bookkeeping department, had mercifully stayed out of the secretarial pool. All in all, Lauren thought, as she pulled a finished letter from her typewriter, things had gone rather well. If only her job were a bit more interesting, perhaps she'd stop thinking about Matt Chandler. What she needed was the kind of work that would occupy her mind as well as her shorthand pad.

'Lauren? Have you finished with those memos I gave you this morning?'

She looked up at her supervisor and nodded. 'Yes, Mrs Lane, I left them on your desk a while ago. I was just about to do some filing.'

'Before you get started, Lauren . . .' The woman perched on the edge of the desk and smiled. 'I just had coffee with your mother, dear. She tells me you learned all about using word processors in business school.'

Lauren's cheeks reddened. 'Yes, I did. But she shouldn't have——'

'I'm glad she did, Lauren. I'm sure I must have read that in your file, but I guess I'd forgotten. I don't know a thing about those machines,' she added, leaning forward and dropping her voice dramatically, 'and neither do the other girls. Well, they just got one upstairs, and the girl who was trained to use it is out sick. Would you mind going up there, Lauren? I know you want to get to your filing, but . . .'

'I'd be delighted to help out upstairs, Mrs Lane,' Lauren said quickly. 'I'm not sure their word processor is the kind I'm used to, but I'd like to give it a try.'

Minutes later, she hurried down the third-floor corridor, heading for the room to which she had been directed. The corridor was lined with offices, their doors opened wide, and the low hum of typewriters and voices gave the place a sense of direction and purpose that seemed lacking in the secretarial pool. The atmosphere reminded her of the San Francisco firm in which she'd worked for a couple of months as part of her training. Her steps quickened. If the word processor was one with which she was familiar, perhaps she could spend the rest of the day on this floor. It would certainly be preferable to the dull routine that awaited her downstairs.

The door to the office at the end of the corridor was ajar; she could see the word processor standing on a desk in front of the window, and she breathed a sigh of satisfaction as she saw its familiar keyboard and video screen. It was, indeed, the kind she had used in school. A man was bent over it, a building maintenance man, she thought, judging by his blue jeans and workman's shirt. His back was to her, but she could hear him muttering under his breath as he poked and prodded at the silent machine. A smile flickered across her face and then faded as he began to push against the table on which the processor stood.

'Don't mistreat it just because you can't figure out how it works,' she said sharply. 'You won't be able to watch a football game on it no matter what you do.'

'Don't you sound so condescending,' he growled, 'although a television set would at least be useful. Anyway, I'm not mistreating it; I'm just going to move it out of the way so I can make room for a typewriter. At least they work without magic incantations.'

Lauren's face had paled at his first words; now, as he turned and faced her, she drew in her breath sharply. It was Matthew Chandler who stood before her. The angry scowl faded from his face, replaced by a slow, delighted smile. A thick lock of dark hair had fallen across his forehead, and he pushed it back, leaving a faint smudge of dirt over his eye.

'Well, this is a pleasant surprise,' he said softly. His eyes drifted over her, moving slowly from her high-heeled pumps to her pale grey dress to the tinted, wire-framed glasses perched on the bridge of her nose. 'I like you with glasses on. I'm glad to see you didn't leave them in your car this time.' She stared at him blankly, and he grinned. 'Stop looking as if you'd seen a ghost, Lauren! This is my office.'

'Your office?'

'Nobody else's,' he laughed. 'It certainly took you long enough to find your way up here.'

She stiffened under his gaze. 'What is that supposed to mean?' she asked coolly. 'My supervisor only gave me this assignment a few minutes ago. I got here as quickly as I could."

'Not quite, Lauren. You're about two weeks late. I've been hoping to see you since the dance.'

There was a rush of colour to her cheeks, and she turned away from his piercing stare.

'I've been hoping to see you, too,' she said crisply. 'I wanted to set the record straight. That night . . .'

'Why didn't you return my phone calls?' Matthew interrupted.

'Phone calls?' she echoed dully.

'Phone calls,' he repeated, moving towards her. 'I called the next morning and again that night.'

She closed her eyes and shook her head, knowing instinctively that this was her mother's handiwork.

'I told you not to bother, remember? You knew how I felt . . .'

He laughed softly, just the way he had in the

locked storeroom. 'Yes, I did. That kiss told me everything I needed to know."

Anger and humiliation flooded through her, and she spun around to face him.

'Look here, Mr Chandler . . .'

'Such formality!' he teased softly. 'The last time we were together, you called me Matt.'

Her face felt as if it were ablaze. 'Mr Chandler,' she repeated with careful deliberation, 'I came here to operate a word processor.'

'Lauren . . .'

'But I'm afraid I won't be able to do that, now that I know this is your office. I'll tell Mrs Lane to send someone else.'

'There is no one else,' he said quickly. 'Mrs Lane already told me she had only one typist with the necessary training.'

Of course, he was right, Lauren thought unhappily. Well, she would just tell her supervisor she couldn't work for Matt Chandler. She'd tell her— what on earth could she tell her, that would make any kind of sense? The word processor—she'd say it wasn't the kind she was familiar with. She'd say it was too complex, too difficult . . .

'You didn't get my messages. I'll bet you didn't get my letter either,' he said suddenly.

'Letter?' she repeated. 'What are you talking about?'

'I had to leave on business a couple of days after the dance, and wrote to you, Lauren.' He shook his head at the surprised look that came over her. 'I suspected your mother might not have told you I called, but does she always censor your mail?'

'Look, my mother has nothing to do with this, Mr Chandler. She knows how I felt about you. She . . .'

He laughed softly. 'Does she? I'd have thought you wouldn't have told her everything.'

'You're insufferable!' Lauren hissed. 'And I'm not going to subject myself to any more of this!' She tossed her head and turned away from him. 'I'm going back downstairs and tell Mrs Lane that . . .'

'Go on, Lauren,' he said pleasantly. 'Just what are you going to tell her? That you can't work for the Vice-President of the company? That you're going to disregard an assignment you've been given . . .'

'Mr Chandler——'

'You're going to disregard it,' he repeated, 'and leave me to type my own report.' He sighed dramatically and shook his head. 'That's going to look terrific on your probationary job review.'

Lauren clenched her fists and took a deep breath. 'You're twisting this around to suit yourself!'

'I'm simply stating the facts, Lauren. I'm afraid your supervisor will be less than pleased.'

Fighting back her anger, she spun around and faced him squarely. 'Are you threatening me?'

Matt's face wore a look of wounded innocence. 'Of course not,' he said carefully. 'I'm just telling you what's going to happen once you walk out the door.' He smiled slightly and ran his fingers through his hair again. 'Of course, if that upsets you, I could simply tell Mrs Lane the truth—that you don't trust yourself alone with me, considering what happened the last time we were together.'

'Where's the report you want typed?' she demanded grimly, choking back all the names he deserved to be called. 'The sooner I get started, the sooner I can get out of here.'

His footsteps echoed softly on the wide-planked oak floor as he walked towards her and she stiffened, half expecting to feel the touch of his hand, but he moved past where she stood and gestured towards the desk.

'There are my notes,' he said casually. 'See if you can pull them together into something my father can understand. I don't think you'll run into any problems, but if you do . . .' Her eyes widened as he started to unbutton his shirt. 'Don't look so startled,' he said, grinning at her. 'I'm only going to take a shower and wash off some of this grime. I've been out in the vineyards all morning. Of course, if you're in a rush, you can always come in and ask me to clarify things for you.'

Her glance dropped to the undone buttons on his shirt and she blushed. 'I'm sure I'll manage,' she said stiffly, turning her back on him and shuffling blindly through the pages on the desk. She drew a sigh of relief when she finally heard the door to his private office close behind him.

The notes were concise and clear, and she had no difficulty organising them into a coherent outline. Apparently Matthew Chandler had spent the past two weeks abroad, visiting several of the great vineyards of France. There were detailed descriptions of the white wines of the Loire Valley and the Champagne district, and the grapes that had produced them. Matt had drawn comparisons between some of the grapes grown by Chandler and those originating at several French wineries. The names of the stock were all familiar to Lauren, although some of the conclusions Matt had drawn were not, and she began to nod her head as she proof-read the material displayed on the screen before her.

'You conquered the beast, I see.'

His voice startled her, and she looked up from the

screen. 'It isn't difficult,' she said stiffly. His dark
hair was damp and curling from the shower, and
he'd changed into another, even more faded pair of
jeans and a cotton shirt. Crazily, she found herself
wondering how he could look handsome in jeans as
well as the dinner jacket she had first seen him
wearing, and she turned back to the machine in front
of her, hoping he hadn't seen the speculation in her
eyes. 'Do you want to check this before I print it?'

'Can you run the whole thing on the screen?' he
asked, and she nodded her head. He bent over the
back of her chair as her fingers flew across the
keyboard. 'Okay, then, let's take a look.'

Lauren could feel the warmth of his breath on her
neck as he read the outline over her shoulder. Her
hands trembled on the keyboard and she snatched
them away and dropped them into her lap. God,
what was the matter with her? she wondered angrily.
She knew what he was—one of those awful people
her mother made up to. He was even worse than that,
she reminded herself. He'd played with her two
weeks before, enjoyed himself at her expense. Even
her mother, with all her foolish dreams for Lauren,
had warned her against this man. Then why this
schoolgirl reaction? Why was her heart pounding?
He hadn't touched her, hadn't even tried to, and yet
her body seemed to be tingling in anticipation . . .

'How do you call up the next page?' he asked, and
she forced herself to lift her hand and touch the
proper key. His hand closed lightly over hers and she
flinched. 'Is that all there is to it?' he asked, and she
nodded again, pulling her hand free of his.

'Perhaps if I got out of your way . . .' She started to
rise from the chair and he placed his hand on her
shoulder.

'You're not in my way,' he said firmly, and Lauren sat back, the feel of his hand like a brand burning through her thin cotton dress. Finally, after what she knew must have been only minutes but seemed like hours, he sighed and straightened up behind her.

'It's fine, Lauren. In fact, it looks as if you improved on my notes. I thought I left out the soil acidity level needed for Pinot Noir grapes. I was going to check it in the reference room.'

She blushed and nodded. 'Yes, I saw the note you'd made. But I knew the level required, so I put it in. I hope that's all right.'

Matt chuckled softly. 'Don't tell me you not only know how to work this damned machine but you also know something about wine? That would be too much to hope for.'

'I grew up in San Jacinto,' she said stiffly. 'Why wouldn't I know about wine? Besides, I took a couple of night courses in vinification and viticulture when I was going to school in San Francisco.'

'You mean you actually studied wine-making and grape-growing? Lauren Webster, you've just condemned yourself to an afternoon spent toiling in the vineyards! Don't look so upset,' he laughed. 'I won't make you do any manual labour, I promise. I have to go up into the north acreage, and I planned on taking a tape recorder with me.' He smiled and again his eyes swept over her. 'You can't blame me for preferring you to a machine, can you?'

'Mr Chandler . . .'

'Matt,' he said quickly. 'This is a very informal office, Lauren. You don't want to be the only person in the building who calls me Mr Chandler, do you?'

For a second, the thought of spending the rest of the day with him filled her with pleasure. There was no accounting for it, but something quickened within her whenever he was near. Still, she would not make the same mistake twice: she'd been a fool and she had learned her lesson. She took a deep breath and got to her feet.

'Mr Chandler ... Matt,' she corrected herself quickly, before he could, 'I have work to do downstairs. I'm sure you can manage without me.' He wasn't even listening, she thought furiously, watching as he stuffed papers into a leather briefcase. 'My supervisor . . .'

'I'll call down and let her know you won't be back,' he said, snapping closed the latch on the briefcase. He looked at his watch. 'It's almost noon. That gives us the whole afternoon to work. But you can't go into the fields dressed like that,' he added, glancing at the grey cotton dress and flimsy high-heeled shoes. 'Why don't I drive you home so you can change into something more suitable?'

Her head was spinning. Suppose she agreed to go with him. It was almost noon, he'd said. Her mother would be home for lunch today, waiting for some sort of delivery. What could she say to her? That she was just following orders?

'Lauren?'

She raised her head and looked at him. He was smiling, holding his hand out to her, and suddenly she knew she wanted to spend the next hours with him, without any interference from her mother, without questions and lectures afterwards. What harm could come of an afternoon spent taking notes in the vineyard? This was business.

'You don't have to take me home,' she quickly. 'I . . . I have tennis shoes in the boot of my car.'

Again, she had that curious feeling that he knew

what she was thinking, just as he had that night on the terrace. He studied her in silence, then he smiled.

'Okay,' he said lightly, 'we'll pick up your shoes on the way out. Look, I have an extra pair of jeans and a couple of shirts in my office. Why don't you go in and try them on?' His smile broadened. 'Of course, they won't be a perfect fit . . .'

The thought of wearing his clothing, of having it against her skin, made Lauren blush.

'I couldn't,' she answered quickly. 'Anyway, it isn't necessary.' Her glance followed his to the fragile fabric of her dress and she sighed with resignation. There wasn't a way in the world she could tramp through the narrow rows between the vines without ruining it. 'All right,' she said at last, 'I'll change and come with you.'

'That's good,' he said quietly.

His simple response seemed somehow inappropriate. She had, after all, agreed only to change her clothing and do the job her employer had asked of her. His eyes met hers, and the unspoken message in their dark blue depths told her instantly that his answer had nothing to do with business.

But then neither did her own feeling of excitement.

CHAPTER THREE

MATT's jeep, with the distinctive Chandler logo painted on its sides, bounced along the dusty road that wound through the flat, rich earth of the Napa Valley. Lauren sat stiffly in the passenger seat, staring straight ahead at the low, rounded hillside of the northernmost section of the vineyards. What was she doing out here? she thought. Her hastily made decision to spend the afternoon alone with Matt made no sense. In fact, it had been foolish—almost as foolish as the outfit she was wearing. She felt ridiculous dressed in an old sweatshirt of his and a pair of faded jeans rolled up almost to mid-calf, although he'd greeted her hesitant appearance from his private office with a delighted smile.

'You look terrific,' he'd assured her. 'Like a kid dressed in grown-up clothing.'

And that was precisely how she felt as the jeep climbed to the top of the hill. Certainly, an adult wouldn't have changed into this silly outfit and gone traipsing off into the fields with someone like Matt Chandler. She glanced at him out of the corner of her eye. Had he sensed the confused welter of emotions she had felt in his office? If he had, there was no telling what he might expect of her. Her eyes moved quickly over his hands lying on the steering wheel. What if he touched her as he had that night? What if he tried to draw her into his arms and kiss her? The thought sent a warm tremor through her. Would that dizzying sweetness overtake her again, or would she be able to remind herself of how she felt about the Matthew Chandlers of this world?

'A penny for your thoughts, Lauren.'

She shook her head and forced a smile to her lips. 'You'd be overpaying,' she said lightly. 'I was just daydreaming about . . . about those notes of yours. It sounded as if you were considering planting some new stock.'

He smiled. 'I'd like to. I saw some French Sauvignon Blanc cuttings that would do well in this soil and climate. In fact, one of the vintners I met with last week has agreed to sell me some.'

Lauren shifted in her seat and faced him. 'And you think it would improve what Chandler produces?'

'I know it would,' said Matt without hesitation. 'We've been improving our white wines the past couple of years, but those grapes would add a smoothness ours still lack. Not that our wines aren't exceptional already . . .'

A hint of a smile touched Lauren's lips. 'You don't have to convince me,' she said evenly. 'I like California whites—some of them are as good as the French.'

'Some of them are better,' he said defensively. 'It's just that the French label . . .' He glanced at her and grinned. 'Are you trying to bait me, Miss Webster?'

Lauren smiled as he pulled the jeep under the overhanging branches of a tall oak standing like a lonely sentinel under the hot sun at the entrance to the vineyard.

'I couldn't resist. Of course some of our wines are better. Still, that's an argument that's gone on for ever, hasn't it?' Her smile broadened. 'My grandfather thought that the difference between a good wine and a great one was the amount of love that had gone into making it. And the French, he said, were experts on love, while Americans were experts on efficiency.'

Matt swung out of the jeep and bent to scoop up a handful of earth. 'Your grandfather sounds like a sensible man. Too bad my father doesn't see things the same way.'

'I heard he was going to retire.'

'Only from the day to day operation of the place, not from long-term planning. We've already started arguing over a new filtration system. He insists we'll save money by eliminating sediment from the wine because then the bottles won't have to be moved or stored as carefully.'

'My grandfather used to say that the sediment in a bottle of good wine was its soul, and without a soul, the true essence of the wine was lost.'

'Your grandfather must have been one hell of a vintner. Did he grow grapes in this valley?'

Lauren gazed down at the land sprawled below them. Rows of dark green vines stretched to the rolling hills beyond. Clusters of small, unripened grapes hung from the carefully pruned vines like pale emeralds. By harvest time, in October, they would be dark and heavy with juice, ready to yield their rich sweetness to the pressing vats.

'Grandpa owned twenty acres, years before I was born. He lost most of it during the depression. There was just enough land left for a handful of vines, and he tended them and made wine until the day he died. I used to love to work the fields with him, and pick the grapes . . .'

'You sound as if you loved him a lot.'

'I did,' Lauren said softly. 'My father died before I was born, and Mother lost touch with his family. She was always busy working, so I ended up spending a lot of time with my grandfather.' She smiled wistfully. 'I don't think she approved of all the time I spent in the fields. She thought it was unladylike.'

Matt sifted the particles of dirt through his fingers and chuckled softly. 'I know what you mean. My father still thinks I spend too much time out here and not enough in the office. When I was a kid, I used to plead with him to let me stay home from school during harvest-time. Sometimes I'd pretend I was sick, and than I'd sneak out into the vineyards with the pickers. I could never figure out why the grapes didn't taste as good as they smelled.'

'Oh, but the juice pressed from them was delicious,' she said, getting out of the jeep and standing beside him. 'Grandpa always laughed at me—he'd tease me about the purple moustache I grew each October. But my mother hated it. I guess the stains on my face and clothes reminded her of how much land we once had and how little was left . . .' Her voice trailed off into silence. 'That was a long time ago.'

'What happened to your grandfather's land?' Matt asked quietly.

Lauren shrugged her shoulders. 'It's gone. There were only two acres left when he died, and my mother had to sell it to pay back taxes. It isn't as tragic as it sounds,' she added quickly, seeing the look on Matt's face. 'After all, what can you do with a handful of grapevines?'

Matt grinned ruefully. 'I'm almost afraid to ask . . . Did my father buy those two acres?'

She burst out laughing. 'No, of course not. The Alden Winery acreage backed right up to Grandpa's land, and they bought it. Why would you ask that?'

'Well, it might explain why your mother was so angry when she found us together.'

'It had nothing to do with that,' she said.

'Then what was it?' he asked quietly. 'You acted as if I'd become someone else, once you knew my name was Chandler. Until then, there was magic between us. Both of us knew it.'

She had almost forgotten her distrust of him while they talked, but his words brought reality back with chilling harshness. Their easy conversation had been meaningless. It had only been a prelude to the moment when he could remind her of the way she had behaved the night they met. Then, it had been fireworks and poetry. Today, it was childhood memories and wine. Did he really think she hadn't learned anything?

'I thought we came out here to do some work,' she said stiffly.

'Yes, but you know that's not the only reason...'

'It's the only reason I came with you, Mr Chandler. We'd better get started. My working day ends at five o'clock.'

She turned back to the car and snatched his briefcase and her shorthand pad from the floor, angrier with herself than with him. Make up your mind, Lauren, she thought furiously. You can't go on hating him one minute and being attracted to him the next.

'Look,' she said quickly, 'you were going to manage with a tape recorder. Why don't I take the jeep back to the office and send a messenger out to meet you with one ... What are you doing?'

'Getting our lunch,' he answered calmly, hoisting a wicker basket from the jeep. 'While you were changing your clothes, I raided my office refrigera-

tor. You have to have lunch, Lauren. Your contract
calls for it, and as you just pointed out, this is a
working day for you. Why don't you spread this
blanket under the tree while I unpack?'

She caught the wool blanket he tossed her
automatically, and watched in bewildered silence
while he opened the basket.

'We've got Monterey Jack cheese and French
bread.' He grinned and looked at her. 'And wine, of
course. Chandler estate-bottled Chardonnay. I'd
have preferred white Bordeaux, but it wasn't chilled.
Here, give me that blanket,' he added, taking it from
her. 'I suppose I shouldn't have asked you to do that;
your contract calls for clerical work only, doesn't it?
If you'll just sit down and hold out those glasses . . . I
know you usually have lunch a bit earlier than this,
but I'm sure I can square it with your union . . .'

'Stop it!' she whispered angrily.

He glanced up and stared at her with a look of total
innocence on his face.

'Stop what? You're working, aren't you? You're
entitled to sixty minutes for lunch, or is it forty-five?
I can never remember . . .'

'You've made your point,' she said, the colour
mounting swiftly to her cheeks. 'You're my employer, and I have no choice but to take your orders.
That's how you got me out here in the first place.'

'Lauren . . .'

'But enough is enough. I'll take your dictation, but
I won't play your games.' She took a deep breath and
lifted her chin. 'Times have changed, Mr Chandler.
You can't force me into anything, so you can just stop
your not-so-subtle reminders of who you are and who
I am. I don't want your lunch, I don't want this
assignment, and I don't want to see you again. If that

means I'll lose my job, so be it.'

She felt the sting of angry tears in her eyes and turned away from him before he could see them. The winery was only a couple of miles away; she could walk that distance in less than an hour. There was no one but herself to blame for this, she thought furiously, but this was the end of it. The man was an arrogant bully, who thought he could cow her into his bed.

She kicked his briefcase aside and started towards the road, ignoring him as he called her name. Her footsteps quickened as she heard his feet scuffing the dust behind her.

'Damn it, Lauren,' he growled, grasping her shoulders, 'it's time we talked this thing out.'

'We have nothing to say to each other,' she said curtly, trying to pull free of his grip.

'We certainly do,' he insisted, forcing her to turn and face him. 'I wasn't playing games, at least not the kind you described, and you know it.'

'What I know is how carefully you set this up,' she snapped angrily, her eyes flashing as they met his. 'And you made quite a point of reminding me that I work for you and have to take your orders.'

'I didn't set this up. How the hell would I know you were the secretary Mrs Lane would send to my office? And you know damned well I was only teasing you about losing your job. You wanted to come with me. I just gave you a reason you could live with.'

'I wanted to come with you?' she asked incredulously. 'You are the most conceited, arrogant person that ever lived, Matthew Chandler! Why would I want to go with you? I don't even like you. I'm only here because it was my job.'

'You know, I think you've even got yourself believing that,' he said harshly. 'Don't turn away from me,' he added, his fingers biting into her shoulders. 'The truth is, you wanted to be with me, and you're angry with yourself for that. When you started to relax and enjoy yourself, you had to remind both of us that you were here only because you work for Chandler Vineyards. Well, it's time you stopped lying, Lauren. You're here because you feel the same thing I feel. Why the hell can't you admit it?'

'I won't even dignify that with an answer,' she said coldly. 'You are precisely what I expected, Mr Chandler, a carbon copy of your buddies at the Club. You think your money, your position, can buy you anything. Well, I'm one thing you can't buy. And you don't like that one little bit, do you?'

His face whitened with anger. 'I'm not anybody's carbon copy, Miss Webster, and I don't buy people. I have no idea who you're comparing me to, but I'm very much my own man. You seemed to think so too, at first.'

'We met under false pretences,' she said stiffly. 'Now, would you please let go of me?'

'What false pretences? I was a man you met at a dance, and you were the loveliest, most natural woman I'd ever met.'

'Is that the sort of woman on your list this year?' snapped Lauren. 'The down-to-earth, pretty type? My mother told me you were a collector; even she didn't want me to get involved with you, and God knows she's been steering me towards your sort for years.'

Matt laughed bitterly. 'Is that what this is all about? Your mother?'

'Just leave her out of this, please. I'd have walked

away from you all by myself as soon as I knew who you were. Now, if you'll let go of me . . .'

But his grasp only tightened, and he shook his head. 'You're really something, you know that? You're a snob. You pre-judge people without even knowing them. Did you expect a Chandler to have horns and a tail?'

'Nothing so overt, Mr Chandler. And don't flatter yourself. You're not alone in that category; I don't like any of your crowd.'

'You didn't feel that way that night, did you?' His hand slipped from her shoulder to the small of her back, and his other hand twisted into her hair, forcing her face up to his. 'When I kissed you . . .'

'I didn't know who you were,' she protested, and he laughed.

'I see. It was all right to kiss a stranger that way, but not Matt Chandler.'

Lauren shook her head in protest. 'No, no . . . you're distorting everything. It wasn't like that . . .'

His fingers tightened in the soft spill of her hair and he pulled her against him.

'Damned right it wasn't,' he said roughly. 'We were strangers only until I took you in my arms, Lauren. And then it was as if we'd known each other a lifetime.'

'Please, don't . . .' Her whispered protest died under the hard pressure of his mouth. She struggled against him, but his arms held her fast. His kiss was wild and punishing, given as much in anger as in passion, and then suddenly it softened and changed, and the tender sweetness she had tried so hard to forget returned. Unwillingly, even as she still fought against him, her eyes closed. His hand slid to the nape of her neck and he gathered her closer to him.

She tried to push him from her, but her hands moved, as if of their own will, up the broad, hard expanse of his chest to his shoulders. She shuddered as he bit gently at her lip, and her mouth opened under the increasing heat of his.

Certainly she had been kissed before; there had even been a man in San Francisco, one who had kissed her and wanted to make love to her, but nothing had prepared her for this spinning whirlpool of desire. All her senses were under attack: her whole being became centred on the honeyed taste of Matt's mouth, the smell of the grass and the grapes, the feel of the thick, curling hair on the back of his neck as her fingers tangled in it. His voice, when he whispered her name against her mouth, was the only sound in her tumbling universe, although the wind was sighing softly through the branches of the great oak tree standing beside them. It was only when she felt his hand beginning to caress her that she finally stirred and pulled her mouth free of his.

'No . . . Matt, please . . .' She felt the brush of his fingertips against the swell of her breast, and then he released her.

'What are you doing to me?' she whispered unsteadily. 'I don't know what you're trying to prove.'

His face was white under its summer tan. 'Don't you?' he asked hoarsely, running his hand through her hair. 'I told you before: something happened when we met, some magic . . .'

'I don't believe in magic,' she said harshly. 'Magic is for books and films, not real life.'

'This is real life. You and I.'

'You and I? What does that mean? I hardly know you.'

'Then get to know me,' he said quickly. 'Don't rely on some stereotype you've got in your head.' A smile flickered across his face. 'I've been told I'm a pretty nice guy.'

'By whom?' she asked stiffly. 'The women you've been involved with?'

He shook his head and put his hands on his hips. 'What the hell did your mother tell you about me? Look, Lauren, I won't pretend I've been a saint.' He smiled wryly. 'I'm thirty-two years old, and I admit I've been around. But the women I've been with wanted the same thing I did.'

'I'm not like that,' she interrupted, and he smiled faintly as he reached out and touched her cheek.

'I know,' he said softly. 'You're not like any woman I ever met. I knew that the first time I saw you. Kissing you, talking to you, just being with you—all of it is special. You feel it, too, I know you do. Why can't you admit it?'

Lauren closed her eyes. 'I'm so mixed up,' she admitted at last. 'I'm not sure of anything.' Her eyes opened and met his. 'And I've never . . . never behaved this way with a man,' she added, her voice faint with embarrassment. 'It's not like me.'

Matt tilted her face up to his and grinned. 'I'm glad to hear it!'

'Don't tease me,' she said unhappily.

'I'm not teasing you, Lauren. I know you have doubts about me, about yourself, but what happened the other night wasn't just the result of moonlight and music.' His voice dropped to a whisper. 'It's midday, and there's no music, yet we still feel the same way. Why can't we acknowledge that? Would it be so wrong if we got to know each other better?'

The feel of his kiss still lingered on her lips. For the

first time, she allowed herself to think that perhaps she'd been too quick to categorise him.

'No,' she sighed, 'I guess it wouldn't.'

'Okay,' he said resolutely, 'then that's what we'll do.' He reached for her again, but she shook her head and stepped back.

'No more,' she said firmly, although her heart was racing and she ached to move into the warmth of his arms and give herself up to his kisses. 'There are other ways to get to know each other.'

Laughter danced in his eyes. 'Ah, but they aren't as much fun! Only joking,' he said quickly, holding his hands up in surrender. 'In fact, I'm going to leave it up to you. I won't kiss you again until you ask me to.'

Lauren answer was swift. 'Why?' she asked suspiciously, blushing when Matt chuckled. 'I mean, that's fine, but what will it prove?'

'You see? How can we get to know each other when you still don't trust me?' He sat down beneath the tree and held his hand out to her. Hesitantly, she put her hand in his and sat down opposite him. 'It will prove,' he said softly, 'that you can trust your instincts, that it's okay to like me even though I'm rich and handsome.'

His face was a study in innocence, and she began to laugh softly.

'Humble, too,' she said.

'Absolutely,' he agreed solemnly, then he grinned. 'And hardworking. Which reminds me . . .' He reached for the bottle of Chardonnay and filled their glasses. 'We'd better have lunch. We've got a lot of work to do this afternoon.' They touched their glasses together and Matt took a sip of wine. 'Not bad,' he said reflectively. 'Well, to be absolutely honest, I had a Chardonnay in Amboise last week that was a bit smoother.'

'That's because the French don't pretend that you can make a varietal wine and use only fifty-one per cent of the grape for which it's named,' Lauren said archly, and Matt burst out laughing.

She smiled at him over the rim of her wineglass, and suddenly he leaned over and put his hand lightly on hers. The quiet intensity in his eyes made the breath catch in her throat.

'Fair warning, Lauren Webster—when you do ask me to kiss you, I'm going to start and never stop.'

All she could think, as she turned away from him in confusion, was that perhaps she wouldn't want him to.

CHAPTER FOUR

LAUREN drove slowly through the quiet streets of San Jacinto, wincing at the sound of her old Ford's noisy silencer. The Saturday morning streets were deserted, but she felt as if a thousand eyes were watching. It was nonsense, she knew—at barely eight a.m., the town was still slumbering, grateful for the night's respite from the muggy August heat. Nevertheless, she sighed with relief as she passed the last few houses and headed towards the open countryside.

Matt had said he would be waiting for her at the winery parking-lot, which was sure to be deserted at this hour on a Saturday morning. As always, it had embarrassed her to ask him to agree to such clandestine arrangements and it had irritated him; she had seen it in the quick narrowing of his eyes and the tensing of his jaw.

'When are you going to tell your mother we're seeing each other?' he'd asked. Then, as if he sensed her discomfort, he ruffled her hair. 'Hey,' he'd added quickly, 'I'm not complaining. Seeing you this way is better than not seeing you at all.'

Lauren decided not to mention her one hesitant attempt to tell her mother they were seeing each other. She had tried to approach the topic with some subtlety by mentioning that she had filled in as Matthew Chandler's secretary for an afternoon. But her mother interrupted at once; she began repeating all her accusations, concluding with the remainder that although Lauren might be unable to avoid him

54

at work, she was never to see him socially.

'Don't tell me what to do, please,' Lauren had bristled.

Her angry response had fanned the flames of an argument that had long smouldered between them. It had ended without any resolution, as it always did, when her mother, her face a mask of hurt and incredulity, captured the last word for herself.

'I love you, child,' she'd said, as if that explained her right to command Lauren's life. 'Everything I do is for you.'

Lauren's determination to stand up to her had crumbled.

She slowed her car and swung into the Chandler parking-lot. She knew Matt would be waiting for her, his car hidden from inquiring eyes between a storage shed and a loading dock, just as it had been whenever they had met during the past month. Each time she saw him, the happiness she felt was almost enough to wipe out the guilt that tugged at her soul. She drove to the rear of the winery and smiled when she saw him leaning against his low-slung Corvette.

'Good morning,' he said, leaning into the open window of her car and smiling at her. 'No, wait,' he added quickly when she started to open the door. 'I just want to make sure of something . . .' The smile faded and was replaced by a look of such seriousness that Lauren blushed.

'What?' she said uncomfortably. 'Come on, Matt, what is it?' Automatically, she ran her fingers through her hair, smoothing down a few errant strands. Was there a smudge on her cheek, perhaps?

Finally he shook his head. 'No,' he said positively, 'I'm not crazy. I've been sitting here waiting for you, and I got to thinking that maybe I'd imagined that face. But you're every bit as pretty this morning as you were last night.'

Lauren punched his arm lightly. 'Will you stop teasing me?' she said, pushing the door open. 'You make me uncomfortable!'

'I'm not teasing,' he said, helping her into his car. 'The truth shouldn't make you uncomfortable.'

She sighed and shook her head. 'Please, let's not talk about me and the truth in the same breath. My mother was awake when I left. I told her I was going to visit a girl friend in San Francisco and she told me to have a good time. The least I expected was to start dodging lightning bolts! I hate myself for lying.'

'We could solve that problem, you know. All I have to do is go to your house and ring the doorbell.' He took her hand in his and squeezed it lightly. 'Your mother would open the door, and I'd say, "Good morning, Mrs Webster. I've come to call for your daughter . . ." '

'. . . and Mother would say, "You're not welcome here, Mr Chandler," and I'd come racing down the stairs and tell her she was wrong, and before you knew what had happened, she and I would be in the midst of a fight over what right she has to interfere in my life.' Lauren tossed back the long blonde hair that fell softly around her face and smiled ruefully. 'Does picking me up at home still sound like such a great idea?'

'Maybe it's time you settled that, once and for all,' Matt suggested as he backed the Corvette from its parking space. 'You don't want her to tell you how to live your life for ever, do you?'

'No, of course not, but she doesn't see it that way.' Lauren shook her head and sighed. 'I know you're right, Matt, but I'm all she has. She's given me everything.'

'Guilt isn't a reason for a relationship, Lauren,' he said softly. 'Loving her is one thing, but letting her make you feel as if you owe her something is quite another.'

'She doesn't make me feel that way,' Lauren said quickly. 'I just don't want to hurt her, that's all.'

The car purred softly as they swung out of the lot. 'Yeah, but what about hurting yourself? You have the right to live your life . . .'

'I am living it,' she answered firmly. 'I guess it's hard for you to understand, Matt, but it's impossible for me to turn my back on her. She has no one else.'

'I'm not asking you to turn your back on her, for God's sake,' he said in exasperation, 'I'm simply telling you that we're a little old to be sneaking around like two kids.'

'We don't have to sneak around,' Lauren said stiffly. 'This was your idea, Mr Chandler. I'm not the one who suggested we see each other. I'm not the one who insisted we meet. I'm not . . .'

Matt wrenched the wheel hard to the right and pulled on to the narrow shoulder of the road.

'Listen to me,' he said tightly, grasping her shoulders. 'You want to see me every bit as much as I want to see you. You know you do. But you were willing to let your mother come between us before we even got started.' His grip loosened and he took a deep breath. 'Look, all I'm trying to say it that I'd like to have a real old-fashioned date. The kind where I come to the door and ring the bell and hand your mom a box of chocolates . . .'

'You wouldn't do it unless you wanted to wear them,' Lauren said with a smile. 'Are you certain you never had a run-in with her?'

Matt shrugged his shoulders and pulled on to the road again. 'I told you, I worked in her department for a couple of months when I was learning the business. We never said anything more than hello and goodbye.'

'She says the only thing you learned was the telephone number of one of her clerks.'

They turned on to the winding coast highway that clung precariously to the great cliffs rising beside the ocean. Wispy tendrils of fog lay across the narrow road, surrounding them in milky opalescence.

'I don't even remember any clerk,' Matt said helplessly. 'What did she do—keep notes?'

'How about a little redhead in shipping? Mom says you dropped the clerk for her.'

'For God's sake, Lauren, all that was years ago,' he said angrily. He sighed and ran his fingers through the shock of dark hair that had fallen on his forehead. 'Anyway, I've been the soul of propriety since we met, haven't I?'

'Do I detect a note of complaint, Mr Chandler?' she asked softly.

He reached across the console and took her hand. 'Damned right,' he said lightly. 'I want to get on with my lustful plans. You see, I have this wild, lascivious dream in which I pick you up at your home in full view of your mother and take you to the San Jacinto Inn for dinner. By the next day, the whole town is buzzing with dirt about Lauren Webster and Matthew Chandler dating publicly and violating the sacred Evelyn Webster Moral Code.'

'You're insane!' Lauren laughed.

'I must be,' he agreed with a smile. 'But you've got to admit, it's a great idea.'

It certainly was, she thought, settling back into the bucket seat. Not that she'd expected to feel this way. In fact, the first time she had agreed to meet Matt for dinner, she had told herself it would be their first and last date. The only way she could make any sense out of her feelings was to tell herself that what she felt for him was an infatuation that would die a natural death once they had spent a few hours together. After all, moonlight and fireworks weren't an everyday backdrop, and even their impromptu picnic had been unusual. She had told her mother she was going into San Francisco to have dinner with a friend, comforting herself with the assurance that it wasn't a lie so much as it was an evasion.

Deliberately, she had asked Matt to take her to an unattractive little Italian restaurant near the school she had attended. And at her urging, they had gone to see a poor revival of a dull play. But somehow, she remembered, stealing a glance at him, the evening had been wonderful. The restaurant had been transformed by his presence. Its dreary furnishings became romantic and its menu intriguing rather than predictable. The play seemed to sparkle with wit; they laughed at nuances no one else in the half empty theatre noticed. At the final curtain, they applauded with such enthusiasm that finally the rest of the bewildered audience joined in and the surprised cast emerged for a bow.

And then last night, they had simply driven into San Francisco and wandered through the streets. Eventually, they had squeezed into a crowded little coffee shop and sipped cups of fragrant *cappuccino* while they listened to a sallow-faced young man read his poems to the not-terribly-attentive audience. Afterwards, they'd walked along the beach, picking

out constellations in the blaze of stars high above the
black water, talking about everything, even discov-
ering their shared passion for old science fiction
movies.

And every time, Matt had taken her home—or as
close to home as she'd let him get—and done nothing
more than say good night. Her mother would
probably never believe it, Lauren thought, glancing
at him, but so far Matt Chandler had turned out to be
even more wonderful than she'd sensed the night
they had met. He was charming and sexy, and more
than that, he was funny and sensitive and like no
other man she knew.

'I'll bet I know exactly what you're thinking,' he
said suddenly.

Lauren felt her face redden. 'I hope you can't,' she
said in a bantering tone. 'I'd hate to think I'd lost my
privacy.'

Matt looked over at her and chuckled. 'Interesting
possibility, hmm? I'll be damned, Miss Webster—
you're blushing! What on earth could you have been
thinking?'

She shifted in the bucket seat. 'You tell me,' she
said archly. 'Didn't you just say you would?'

'All I meant was that you're probably wondering
why we're driving towards the city since I said we
were going to the beach today.' A mischievous grin
tilted the corners of his mouth. 'Why do I get the
feeling your thoughts weren't half so uncomplicated
as that?'

'I was beginning to wonder,' said Lauren, deliberately ignoring the rest of Matt's remark. She nodded
at the soaring arch of the Golden Gate Bridge rising
like a ghostly apparition from the fog. 'I thought
we'd be driving up the coast to North Cove Beach.'

'Did I say we were going to North Cove?' he asked mysteriously.

'No, but you said to bring a bathing suit.'

'And did you?'

'I'm wearing it under my clothes. But . . .'

'Good.' He glanced at her and smiled. 'Weren't you worried about being seen at a place so close to San Jacinto? Anyway, I know a much nicer place than North Beach.'

'In San Francisco? I can't think of any . . .'

'And you'll get the chance to meet the lady who's been the centre of my life for the past few months.'

Lauren's eyes widened in disbelief. 'The what?' she repeated slowly.

'I broke a date with her last night so that I could see you. I warn you, she's liable to be annoyed with you.'

He had to be joking, she thought, staring at his impassive profile. But he was still talking, assuring her that they were all going to have a wonderful day together. He smiled at her again, and his voice droned on as pleasantly and casually as ever, but she had no idea what he was saying. His words were nothing but an incomprehensible background to her growing rage.

It was impossible to listen to another word. 'What on earth makes you think either of us would want to meet the other?' she interrupted coldly.

'Come on,' he said teasingly, reaching across the console and ruffling her hair, 'you know you're curious. You want to see the competition you edged out, don't you?'

She edged away from his touch. 'I didn't know I was in a contest,' she said stiffly. 'I assure you, I'm not the least bit interested.'

Matt flashed her a reassuring smile. 'Don't be silly,' he said in the soothing tone one would use with a child. 'You'll like each other.'

Lauren moved as far from him as she could within the narrow confines of the sports car and stared straight ahead. So much for Mr Wonderful, she thought grimly. What incredible arrogance! Did he really think she cared about his old girl-friends? What did he expect them to do, once he'd introduced them? Shake hands? Fight over him? Her shoulders stiffened. Hadn't he said something about the wonderful time they'd all have together? Heaven only knew what he meant by that!

They turned on to a narrow road leading towards the water. It curved around an arm of the bay, ending finally at a small marina. The fog was lifting rapidly under the steady heat of the sun, and the dark blue water gleamed with refracted light. Sleek sailboats bobbed gently at their moorings, their tall masts piercing the cloudless sky. It was a picture that might have been offered by the Chamber of Commerce, but all Lauren noticed as Matt pulled into a parking space was a brief flicker of movement on one of the boats. She stiffened as a tall, honey-skinned brunette in a white bikini rose languidly from a deckchair and smiled in their direction.

'Okay,' she said in clipped tones, 'I've seen your friend. Now take me home.'

He looked at her in surprise, his smile fading as he saw her flushed, angry face.

'Hey,' he said softly, reaching out and touching her cheek, 'what is it?' He followed her gaze as it went, unwillingly, to the brunette, and burst out laughing.

'I don't think it's funny,' she said with tight lipped fury.

'Lauren, sweet, you're looking at the wrong lady.' Gently, his fingers cupped her chin and he eased her head to the left. 'Lauren Webster, meet the *Lovely Lady*.'

Her eyes widened in surprise. Ahead, rising and falling with the gentle swell of the waves, a sailboat gleamed in the sun, her name spelled out in gold letters.

'You mean . . . the boat? That's the lady you . . .' She closed her eyes and shook her head. 'Matt, you're awful. How could you do that to me?'

'How was I to know my neighbor would time things so well?' His grasp tightened and he turned her face to his. 'Did you really think I'd introduce you to some woman I'd been involved with?'

'No . . . yes . . . well, you sounded so serious,' she said miserably. 'I don't know what I thought.'

A slow, teasing smile lit his face. 'I'll be damned,' he said softly. 'You were jealous, weren't you?' She shook her head and tried to turn away, but the pressure of his hand stopped her. 'You were,' he insisted. 'Admit it.'

Lauren took a deep breath. 'I thought you wanted me to meet the *Lovely Lady*,' she said evenly. 'I can't very well do that from the car.'

He stared at her for another few seconds, then he smiled. 'Right you are,' he said lightly. 'Okay, then, let's go aboard.'

She climbed on to the deck gingerly, clutching Matt's hand as if it were a lifeline. The boat—it was a thirty-foot sloop, he told her—seemed a mass of neatly coiled ropes and shining wood. Shading her eyes with her hand, Lauren peered up at the mast. He was talking about the sheets, whatever those were, and telling her all she had to do was cast off the springs. When she arched her eyebrows, he laughed and pointed to the heavy ropes looped around two posts on the dock.

'Those are the springs,' he said patiently, 'and the ropes that control the sails are called sheets.'

Lauren looked doubtful as she tossed the hair back from her face. 'Are you sure you want to do this?'

'You'll be fine; just follow my instructions.'

She cocked her head to the side and sighed. 'Don't say I didn't warn you, Matt. I don't speak sailboat.'

'You will,' he laughed. 'Just remember, I'm the captain and you're the crew. My word is law.'

'Aye, aye, sir,' she answered. 'But try to speak English as often as possible.'

Following his directions, she scrambled across the teak deck to cast off while he eased the boat slowly from the slip and into the open water. Gradually the shoreline receded, until the *Lovely Lady* was moving out on the wind-tossed water of the bay. The breeze was fresh, smelling of the open sea beyond.

'This is terrific,' Lauren said happily.

'But it isn't sailing. As soon as we get a little further out, I'll hoist the sails and shut down the engine. Then you'll really see how great this is.'

She looked at him with apprehension. 'Won't somebody have to steer the boat?' He grinned wickedly and she shook her head. 'Oh, Matt, I couldn't . . . I don't know how . . .'

'Just put both hands on the helm . . . the wheel— that's the way—and keep her in irons, headed into the wind, just the way she was. That's it, Lauren. Be firm but don't fight her; just let her know who's in charge.'

The boat felt like a spirited animal under her hands, willing to obey but eager to break free. Matt moved away from the cockpit, talking to her soothingly, explaining his actions as he unsnapped the sail-cover and winched up the mainsail. It caught the wind and spread majestically. The boat responded at once, surging ahead as the sail filled.

'Easy,' he called, as Lauren's hands tightened on the wheel. 'Just bring her into the wind again. I'll take her in a minute, after I haul up the jib . . . Okay!' he said triumphantly, as he hurried back into the cockpit and his hands closed over hers. 'That wasn't so hard, was it?'

Her eyes shone with pleasure. 'Hard? I was scared stiff that I'd do something wrong—but I didn't, did I? Oh, Matt, this is wonderful!''

The *Lovely Lady* was moving forward eagerly, her lean bow cutting through the water, the sails creaking softly overhead as the waves slapped gently against her hull.

'It's so quiet,' whispered Lauren.

Matt nodded. 'That's the best part of sailing. It's why I've always loved it.'

His hands were still spread over hers on the wheel, and the motion of the boat made her lean back until her body rested lightly against his. It was the closest she had been to him since the day in the vineyard. She drew in her breath at the unexpected contact. He was aware of it, too, she knew. She could feel the tension in him, and his fingers tightened on hers.

'Is the *Lovely Lady* an old friend of yours?' she asked nervously, trying to bridge the tense silence.

Matt chuckled softly. 'A very old friend. She was my first love.'

His arms tightened around her, and she swallowed.

'It's a big boat for one person to handle, isn't it?'

'That's exactly what my father said when I bought her.'

She closed her eyes, trying to ignore the loud hammering of her heart. 'Doesn't your father approve of the *Lovely Lady*?'

Matt's arms dropped to his sides. 'She's not his to approve or disapprove,' he said crisply, moving away from her. 'I'm sure he'd have preferred it if I'd bought a flashy cabin cruiser—some gasoline-guzzling stinkpot that I could have used to entertain clients—but I bought her with my own money, and I sail her in my own time.' He looked at Lauren and smiled wryly. 'My father and I rarely look at things the same way.'

'But you work together?'

'We work for the company,' he said quickly, 'but not together. In fact, we don't even agree on policy. I want Chandler to take some chances, try to break into a better market with some fine wines, but he just wants it to go on the way it has for decades, getting bigger and bigger, owning more land, buying out more small vintners. What he envisages is a dynasty. Here, let me take the wheel for a while,' said Matt suddenly, and Lauren dutifully moved aside. 'The cove we want is just around that point.'

'Then you don't take after your father?'

Matt shook his head. 'He says I take after my mother, that she was a dreamer like me.'

'And was she?'

He shrugged his shoulders. 'I barely remember her, Lauren. She died when I was little. But he's probably right,' he added, his mouth narrowing. 'They must have been very different because I can still remember them arguing all the time. Actually, he argues with everybody, me most of all. That's one of the things I like about sailing—he can't tell me what to do when I'm out here. I have no one but myself to answer to.' His eyes met hers. 'That's why I haven't ever brought anyone with me—until today.'

She could feel herself blush under the intensity of his gaze. 'I get it,' she said with forced gaiety. 'You took me along because I'm a landlubber. How can I argue with you if I don't know what you're talking about?'

Their eyes met and held. The message in his was for her alone, and had nothing to do with sailing. Suddenly she was overwhelmed by the desire to move into his arms and beg him to kiss her.

'You know what I'm talking about,' he said flatly.

She shook her head in confusion and turned away. 'I know that you're starving me,' she said lightly. 'Didn't you promise me a picnic at the beach?'

An eternity seemed to tick away while she waited for his answer. 'I did indeed,' he agreed finally. 'One picnic, coming right up! All you have to do is take the wheel again, while I drop the sails and set the anchor. Well, get to it, woman! The crew has to learn to execute the captain's orders promptly.'

She laughed and did as he asked as they sailed into a calm, half-moon harbour, where gentle waves lapped against a secluded, white-sand beach. Matt secured the boat and wiped his forehead.

'God, it's hot,' he said, pulling off his sweatshirt and tossing it aside. 'Aren't you warm in those jeans?' She nodded her head, uncomfortably aware of his tanned shoulders and chest. 'Well, why don't you strip down to your bathing suit while I raid the galley and get lunch together?'

He clambered down the companionway without waiting for her answer. Hesitantly, she unbuttoned her blouse and slipped it from her shoulders. Why was she so reluctant to take off the rest of her clothing? If they were on a public beach, she'd have thought nothing of it, but here, alone on the calm water of the isolated cove, the simple act of wearing nothing but her modest white *maillot* seemed somehow unnerving. She shook her head and pulled down her jeans. She was being ridiculous, she told herself firmly. They were just two people on a picnic, and in a few minutes Matt would reappear and they'd have a ham sandwich or a hard-boiled egg and a glass of lemonade and . . .

'Lauren? Lunch is ready.'

She whirled at the sound of his voice and stared down into the cabin. The glare of the summer sun made it seem dark below decks; she could barely see him standing at the foot of the ladder, waiting for her.

'I thought . . .' Her voice sounded faint and tentative, and she cleared her throat. 'I thought you said you were bringing lunch on deck.'

Matt shook his head. 'We'll be more comfortable down here, Lauren. It's cooler.'

'But . . .' she glanced over her shoulder at the quiet beach beyond, 'can't we go ashore and have our picnic there?'

He smiled and held out his hand. 'We'll go ashore after lunch, if you like. Wait until you see what I've laid out. You wouldn't really want to load all this into the dinghy, would you?'

Hesitantly, she came down the companionway, ignoring his outstretched hand and moving past him into the galley. The small dining table was laden with cheeses and fruit, pâtés and crusty bread. A bottle of wine stood chilling in a silver ice bucket, and a teak bowl heaped with salad stood beside it. She laughed nervously and waved her hand at the table, trying not to notice how Matt seemed to fill the cabin.

'There's enough food here for a small army!' she protested. 'I don't think I could possibly eat all that. Matter of fact, I don't think I'm hungry at all. Maybe we should just take the dinghy and——'

'What are you afraid of, Lauren?'

'Afraid?' Her laughter sounded forced and brittle to her own ears. 'I'm afraid I'm going to disappoint you, Matt. I mean, here you went to all this trouble, and it turns out I don't have any appetite . . .'

He moved slowly towards her, blocking out the light from the open companionway.

'You could never disappoint me,' he murmured.

'I will if I pass up all this food,' she babbled, backing away from him, until she felt the smooth coolness of the bulkhead behind her. 'Maybe if we went topside for a swim first . . .'

He was so close to her that she could see the pulse beating in his throat. There was a whorl of soft, dark hair on his chest, tapering to a narrow line as it passed his navel and was lost beneath his faded blue jeans. Quickly she raised her eyes to his, looking away when she saw how dark and intense they were.

'Lauren,' he said softly, reaching out to tuck a stray blonde curl behind her ear, 'don't be frightened. I made a promise to you, and I haven't broken it yet, have I?' She shook her head and he smiled. 'I admit, I've been sorely tempted . . .'

'Have you?' she breathed, her voice a throaty whisper.

He nodded his head. 'You know I have. There hasn't been a time we've been together that I haven't wanted to take you in my arms.' His voice dropped to a murmur that was like a caress. 'You don't know what it's been like, Lauren, being with you and not being able to touch you, kiss you . . .'

They were only inches apart in the shadowed cabin. Lauren felt herself swaying, uncertain whether it was because of the rhythm of the sloop or the vertigo within her. She could smell the salt tang of the ocean as it mixed with Matt's own scent and she closed her eyes, as if she could hide from him behind the thick sweep of her dark lashes.

'I do know,' she heard herself say in a small voice. 'It's been hard for me, too. When we were on the beach last night, I hoped you would break your promise . . .'

His hands were on her shoulders, his fingers bruising her skin. 'I told you, Lauren, you're going to have to ask me to kiss you.'

She shook her head, eyes still shut, afraid to look at him. 'That isn't fair,' she whispered.

'You said I had you all mixed up,' he growled. 'You didn't trust me, remember? No, Lauren, the next move is yours.' She felt his hand under her chin, tilting her face up. 'Open your eyes and look at me,' he demanded.

Reluctantly she lifted her lashes. A tremor passed through her as she met his dark blue gaze.

'Tell me what you want,' he insisted, his hand cupping her face.

'Please, Matt . . .'

'Please, what?' he said softly, his hand moving gently to the back of her head and tangling in the wind tossed spill of her hair. 'Tell me, Lauren. Tell me!'

'Kiss me,' she sighed at last, the words a pleading whisper. There was a fleeting look of triumph in his eyes and then his arms were around her and his mouth covered hers.

She knew her kiss was telling him, more than words ever could, everything she had tried to deny to herself the past weeks. It was not enough to feel his body against hers, to taste the sweetness of his mouth. She wanted to melt into him so that nothing could ever come between them. She rose on tiptoe and curled her arms tightly around his neck, wondering at the heated feel of his skin against hers and at how effortlessly their bodies blended together. Matt swung her up into his arms and gently carried her to the starboard bunk.

He whispered her name as his lips touched the long column of her throat, tracing a blazing path of kisses to the rise of her breast. Wordlessly, she ran her fingers through the crisp hair on his chest, feeling the hard muscle beneath, and then his mouth was on hers again, demanding more than before, and she was giving what he asked, opening her lips to his, covering his hand with hers as it found her breast and cupped the swelling flesh. There was no turning back now, she knew, no way to return to the security and safety of the moments before she'd asked him to kiss her. He was the centre of her universe. Without him, she was a doomed star, burning uselessly in a cold void. He was everything she had ever wanted and more than she'd ever imagined. The sudden realisation sent a tremor through her.

'Don't be afraid of me,' he whispered huskily as he felt her tremble in his arms.

'I'm not,' Lauren admitted in a small voice. 'I'm afraid of me—I'm afraid of everything that's happening. It's all too quick and too fast . . .'

'That's the way love is,' said Matt softly. 'There's

nothing very practical or organised about it.'

He bent his head and his mouth took hers, and the possessive need of his kiss thrilled her almost as much as what he had said. And it was true she thought as a tremor of happiness ran through her. She did love him. She had denied it to herself for days—for weeks—but there was no denying it any longer. She loved him and wanted him, and nothing could come between them, nothing . . .

A sudden piercing sound seemed to fill the cabin, and Lauren jumped in fright.

'What was that?' she whispered, her face white with fear. 'Matt?'

'Dammit,' he growled angrily. 'It's an air horn. We must have company; some damned fool wants to make sure we know he's here.' He kissed the tip of her nose and padded to the ladder. 'I'll get rid of him. Wait here for me.'

Lauren swung her feet to the deck and sat up. Quickly she ran her fingers through her hair and touched her hands to her burning cheeks. Wait here, he'd said, but she felt suddenly foolish sitting on the edge of his bed, waiting for him to . . . Quickly she made her way across the cabin and climbed to the cockpit. A large cabin cruiser was moored a few yards from the *Lovely Lady*. Three couples were sprawled on its deck, laughing and gesturing at Matt, who was scowling at them.

'Hello there,' one of the men called in a slurred voice. 'We're having a party. Why don't you folks come on over and join us?' He waved a bottle in the air and almost fell backwards with the effort. 'We got plenty more where this came from!'

'So much for our peaceful afternoon,' growled Matt. 'Just look at those clowns, will you? Drunk as skunks ... I've half a mind to teach them a few things!'

Lauren put her hand on his arm. 'Please, don't,' she said quickly. 'Let's just go.'

He stared at her as if she'd lost her mind. 'Go?' he repeated. 'You expect me to simply let those fools force us out of here?'

'Today was supposed to be a special one, remember?' she pleaded. 'Please, Matt, for my sake—let's lift the anchor or pick it up ...' She saw his mouth begin to twitch and she hurried on, hoping her unintentional mangling of sailing terminology would ease the tension. 'Let's pull it out of the water and sail, okay?'

'Weigh anchor is the phrase you're looking for,' he said, and then he smiled. 'And you're right. This is our day, and I'm not going to let those louts ruin it.'

Lauren smiled in silent agreement. Nothing could ruin the memory of the moments they had spent in the cabin of the *Lovely Lady*. She knew, without question, that her life would never be the same again.

CHAPTER FIVE

'CAN you reach that green blouse at the end of the rack, Lauren? No, no, not that one—the one with the stand-up collar. Yes, that's it. Is it my size?'

'I don't know, Mother. It's all tangled up with the one next to it.'

Lauren looked at her mother across the sale rack of silk blouses. Was it possible she was going to try on something else? Please, she thought, no more. They'd been in this store for at least an hour, first looking at linens and then at shoes and now at these God-awful sale blouses. She sighed as her mother held the green one at arm's length and stared at it, reminding herself that this shopping trip had been her idea. A few hours spent in Macy's on sale day had seemed a small price to pay for the guilt she sometimes felt when she added yet another lie to the crazy quilt she'd created. But it didn't seem to be working. Each minute seemed to drag on for ever, and her patience strained at the leash. And her mother seemed to sense it . . .

'You didn't really have to give up your Saturday for me, Lauren,' Evelyn Webster said in a tone of voice that clearly suggested otherwise. 'Not if you didn't want to.'

'But I wanted to go shopping with you, Mother,' Lauren said quickly. Was she that transparent? she thought, bending towards the blouses so that her mother wouldn't see the sudden rush of colour in her cheeks.

74

'Then why do you keep looking at your watch? If you have something you'd rather be doing today . . .'

An image of Matt waiting for her aboard the *Lovely Lady* flashed through Lauren's mind and she shook her head guiltily.

'No, no, of course not. It's just that you said you wanted to buy a new jacket and we haven't even looked at them yet.'

'I want to look at other things, too. Everything's on sale, you know.' The older woman shoved the blouse back into the rack and moved towards a counter heaped with woollen scarves. 'Didn't you lose the scarf I gave you last Christmas? Let's buy a new one, shall we? It was the same colour as this one—unless you'd prefer the tartan. Either would go with your grey coat.'

'The jackets, Mother, remember?'

Her mother arched her eyebrows. 'I'll get to them in due time, child. I simply thought . . . well, I couldn't purchase this scarf even if I wanted to. There's never a saleswoman in sight when you want one, is there?'

'Does it really matter?' Lauren heard the sharp pitch of her own voice and forced a weak smile to her face. 'I mean, I don't want a scarf anyway.'

'You do need one, though.'

'I don't. I just said that. I . . .' Lauren took a deep breath and shook her head. 'I'm sorry, Mother. We seem to be quarrelling over everything today, don't we?'

'Today?' Evelyn Webster's smile was falsely bright. 'We quarrel all the time lately, Lauren.'

'That's not true, Mother. It's just that you expect me to agree with everything you say.'

'See what I mean? There you are, picking a

fight . . .'

'I am not!' Lauren insisted in a harsh whisper. 'I never do . . .'

'You do, whenever you're home. But of course, you're hardly ever there any more.'

Lauren choked back the automatic protest that rose to her lips. Her mother's words were stiffly critical, but there was a hurt look on her face. Well, why wouldn't there be? The relationship between them had changed drastically. In fact, what Evelyn had said was true. They spent little time together and when they did, as often as not they argued. Just last night, they had clashed when Lauren said she would not attend the Club's Harvest Dance and meet Millie Harrow's nephew who was a doctor or a lawyer or maybe even an Indian chief, as if she gave one good damn.

'. . . don't know what's happened to you, but it upsets me, Lauren. You're not the same child any more. You . . .'

'I'm not a child at all,' snapped Lauren.

Her mother's face fell. 'You're my child,' she said. 'You always will be.'

It was useless to question that kind of reasoning any further. Lauren had tried in the past, and she knew where it would lead. Evelyn would misunderstand every explanation her daughter offered. The only thing that would soothe her would be a declaration of love and loyalty. This time, that would mean agreeing to go to the Harvest Dance, and Lauren had no intention of doing that. But she had no wish to quarrel, either, especially not on one of the increasingly rare days they spent together.

'. . . hurts me when we fight, child. I wish . . .'

'Then let's not fight, Mother.' Impulsively, she

caught her mother's hands in hers. 'Let's go to that little restaurant you like so much—you know, the one down the street—and have some tea.'

'Tea? Now? But we haven't finished shopping. You said so yourself just a minute ago. You were complaining that I haven't even looked at those jackets yet.'

'Yes, yes, I know. But...' Lauren paused and took a deep breath, 'it's true, you know. We don't spend much time together lately. I... I just thought it would be nice if we had a chance to sit and chat.'

Evelyn Webster stared at her daughter for a second and then her expression softened.

'That sounds very nice,' she mused. 'Yes, come to think of it, I could use a cup of tea just about now.'

Moments later, the two women were seated facing each other in a small booth. A pot of tea sat steaming between them. Lauren smiled at her mother as she stirred sugar into her cup.

'Isn't this better than storming the racks in Macy's?'

Her mother smiled in return. 'Much. I'm glad you thought of it, child. Sometimes... sometimes we get so caught up in scurrying from day to day that we forget the important things, don't we?' She glanced around the quiet little restaurant and sighed. 'I used to bring you here when you were little, Lauren. You used to love to get all dressed up in your best dress and your patent leather shoes and drink tea and eat watercress sandwiches...' The older woman's eyes grew misty and she caught her lip between her teeth. 'Of course, you wouldn't remember. It was so long ago...'

I remember, Mother. How could I forget? It was such a special treat to come here—and I loved spending the day with you. It made me feel as if I were all grown up just like you, and we were best friends out for the day.'

Her mother reached for her hand and grasped it. 'We were, child. Oh, we were. We were always so close . . .' Her fingers tightened on Lauren's and she leaned forward. 'Everything's changed lately, hasn't it?' Her words were a mournful whisper. 'I don't know what's happened.'

'Nothing's happened,' Lauren said quickly, although guilt lay in her throat like a gag. 'I . . . I love you, Mother.'

Evelyn Webster smiled faintly. 'I love you, too. But we seem to be at odds with each other all the time.' She glanced down at her cup and sighed. 'I . . . I know I irritate you sometimes, Lauren, with my plans and my fussing, but I simply want you to be happy. You know that, don't you?'

How tired her mother looked, Lauren thought, gazing at her eyes. How many years had it been since she'd had a vacation, a real one? For as long as she could remember, her mother had never gone away, not even for a weekend. There had been money for Lauren's tennis lessons and Girl Scout camp but not for a break in what must have been a tiring, lonely existence. Surely, a woman so devoted to her daughter's happiness would understand the happiness Matt had brought into her life. Once she knew how special he was, that what they shared was unique . . . Lauren took a deep breath.

'I know you want me to be happy, Mother. And . . . and I am. I . . .'

Evelyn's fingers laced through hers. 'That's why I want you to meet the Harrow boy.'

'Oh, Mother!'

'And did I tell you? We've been asked to join the Club. Do you know how few outsiders are accepted into the San Jacinto Country Club? It's quite an honour.'

Lauren pulled her hand free of her mother's. Why had she been so foolish as to think she and her mother could ever understand each other?

'For God's sake—you don't really think we've been accepted, do you? They . . . they tolerate our presence, Mother. We'll never be members. And that's fine with me. I don't like those people.'

'You know, you're as bad as the people you dislike,' said Evelyn quietly, leaning across the table. 'Why do you lump them all together that way? I admit, some of them are a bit unfriendly——'

'Unfriendly? They're clannish and unkind and——'

'Not all of them. Some of them are very nice. Those are the ones I want you to get to know.' Her mother's voice quickened. 'I want you to have all the things you're entitled to, Lauren. That's not so awful, is it?'

Lauren shook her head wearily. 'No one is "entitled" to anything, Mother. Besides, I've told you time and time again that I don't want those things.'

Her mother's eyes narrowed. 'Perhaps we're talking about different things, child. I don't only mean money and clothes and big houses—I mean happiness and . . .'

'You can't mean that, Mother,' Lauren said angrily, her voice rising. She glanced around the quiet teashop and caught her lip between her teeth. 'You don't really think happiness has a price tag on it, do you?' she added in a low voice.

'I don't think it, I know it. Don't look at me as if I were crazy, child! It's much easier to be happy when you don't have to worry about how you're going to pay your bills. And it's certainly simpler to be happy when people look up to you and respect you.'

The two women drew apart as the waitress placed a platter of tiny sandwiches between them, and then Lauren leaned forward again.

'I wouldn't want the kind of "respect" people get just because they have money. That's not respect, anyway, and you know it. It's ... it's *grovelling*!'

'Maybe I'm using the wrong word,' Evelyn Webster said, 'but I know what I'm talking about.' She glanced around and then lowered her voice to a tense whisper. 'Do you think Millie Harrow would have to stand around in a store and look for a salesperson?'

'Oh, for heaven's sake ...'

'All right, scoff at what I say,' her mother said stiffly. 'But you can't deny that money buys things that make life more pleasant. Take the Harrows' daughter, for instance. She's just a couple of years younger than you——'

'I remember her,' Lauren said patiently. 'She was a vapid little thing ...'

'That "vapid little thing",' the older woman said bitterly, 'is off at an expensive university, not working in an office.'

'I'm not ashamed of how I earn my living, Mother. I like my life——'

'Well, I don't,' snapped Evelyn Webster, her face darkening with anger. 'What's the difference between me and the Millie Harrows of this world, hmm? Nothing but an accident of birth, Lauren. Sometimes not even that—my parents were wealthy.

It wasn't my fault that they lost everything before I was born.'

Well, Lauren thought as she stared at her mother, there it was, out in the open at long last. For years, she'd suspected that her mother felt that life had played a cruel jest by denying her the money and privilege that had almost been hers. Now she was certain of it. That was at the core of her mother's determination to break into San Jacinto's tightly knit upper social stratum. If it had been unpleasant to watch Evelyn Webster humble herself before women like Millie Harrow, it was terrible to glimpse the bitter anger and frustration that lay like a cancer festering on her heart. 'When I was growing up,' Evelyn Webster continued, gaining control of herself, her voice once again steady, 'I was caught between two worlds. We had no money, Lauren. I did without a lot of things. But my mother told me what it had been like when she and my father were first married,' she said, a faint, faraway smile on her face. 'I knew all about the country club dances and the teas and the cotillions . . .' She shook her head and her expression hardened. 'Do you think I like humbling myself before people like the Harrows?'

The barely audible question was a surprise. 'I didn't say that,' Lauren mumbled uncomfortably.

'Come on, child. Let's be honest with each other,' the older woman said, leaning across the narrow table. 'Of course I humble myself. Do you think I'm such a fool that I don't know it?'

Lauren shook her head. 'Then why do it? If you know——'

'I can never be anything more than a kind of . . . of interloper, I suppose you'd call it, hovering on the edges of their little world, unless it pleases Millie

Harrow or someone like her to take pity on me and invite me in, and even then, I'm nothing but a curiosity. But you can become part of it, Lauren. You can have everything I didn't.'

They had come full circle, Lauren thought with a sigh. Her mother was bound and determined to marry her off to someone with money—all that had changed was that at least now she knew the reason.

'Look,' she said finally, 'I want you to know that I'm glad you told me how you feel, but I can't do what you want, Mother. I can't just find some wealthy man and fall in love with him.'

Evelyn lifted her chin defensively. 'You make that sound like a social disease! The truth is that it's just as easy to fall in love with a rich man as it is a poor one. Easier, perhaps.'

'Then why did you get so angry when you found me with Matt Chandler?'

The question was out before she could stop it. Evelyn Webster sank back in her seat and raised her hands in defeat.

'We're not really going to go over that again, are we? I told you about him, Lauren. The man's a philanderer.'

'Come on, Mother! No one else seems to think so.'

Her mother's eyebrows arched accusingly. 'Have you been conducting a survey?'

'I only meant that it doesn't make sense,' Lauren said carefully. 'You've pushed me at people like the Chandlers for years, and the one and only time I was interested, you acted as if I'd taken up with Bluebeard!'

'An apt description,' her mother said frostily. 'Matthew Chandler is certainly not a man I'd wish you to become involved with. He is hardly the right sort of person for my daughter.'

'That's ridiculous,' Lauren said impatiently. 'I just told you, nobody thinks he's a villain except you.'

'So you *have* been asking about him!'

'Nobody seems to have the opinion of him that you have. So I wondered why you got so angry when you found us together.'

Her mother shifted uncomfortably. 'I told you the reason, child. He has a bad reputation.'

Lauren shook her head. 'I'm sorry, Mother, but that's not an answer.'

'It certainly is. I don't want you involved with someone who——'

'Is that why you thought you had the right not to let me know he'd tried to get in touch with me?'

The older woman's face flushed. 'Who told you that?' she demanded.

'You were wrong to do that, you know,' said Lauren, her voice taut with quiet intensity. 'I'm capable of making my own decisions!'

'I asked you a question,' her mother repeated.

Lauren took a deep breath. 'The day I worked for Matt, he told me he'd phoned after the dance.'

Her mother's mouth twisted with distaste. 'Matt, is it? How cosy, Lauren!'

'He's a nice man, Mother. I like him.'

'Like him?' Evelyn Webster repeated in a low, disbelieving voice. 'You can't like a Chandler! You can work for one—in this town, it's damned near impossible not to, one way or another, but you don't like them.' She raised her cup to her lips and then set it down on its saucer with a clatter. 'The nerve of that man, phoning my home, sending you letters! As if I'd ever, in a thousand years, permit you to go out with him.'

'Permit me?' Lauren repeated in soft, ominous tones. 'You could hardly stop me. I'm not a child.'

'If you behave like a child, I'll treat you like one.'

'Making my own decisions is not childlike, Mother.'

'Making a fool of yourself with that man was childlike, Lauren.' Her mother took the napkin from her lap and dabbed at her mouth. 'That's the end of the discussion.'

The statement was delivered with such smug complacency that it almost invited challenge. It floated in the air between them like a well-cast fly set in the water to tempt a trout. But Evelyn Webster was no fisherman; she had made what she believed was a final, definitive comment, never expecting Lauren to rise to the bait.

Lauren raised her eyes to her mother's and took a deep breath. 'I don't agree with your opinion of Matt Chandler.'

'I said we wouldn't discuss him any more, child. Anyway, what do you know about the Chandlers? You——'

'I know more than you do,' Lauren snapped. 'You see, Mother, I've gone out with Matt in spite of what you said. And I'm glad I did. All I regret is that I did it on the sly as if I were a . . . a little girl.'

Evelyn's voice was a strained hiss in the quiet restaurant. 'You've done *what*? How could you, Lauren? How could you do this to me?'

'Do what? What have I done that's so awful, Mother?'

'What have you . . .?' Evelyn shook her head. 'I have the highest expectations for you, Lauren. What on earth is the point of wasting your time with a man like that? There are so many other young men in San

Jacinto . . .'

'I haven't met a single one who's as nice as Matthew Chandler.'

'You haven't given yourself half a chance.'

'How can you condemn Matt when you don't even know him?'

Evelyn stared at her in silence, her face grim and narrow-lipped.

'He's a Chandler, isn't he?' she said. 'That's how.'

Lauren pushed her teacup aside and laughed. 'Oh, that really clarifies things,' she said. 'That's a terrific reason for hating Matt!'

'I do not hate the man, Lauren. I simply know that he's not for you.'

'Because he's a Chandler,' Lauren said sarcastically.

Her mother flushed and lifted her hand to her forehead. 'I know that sounds foolish, but I . . . I know the Chandlers, you see. I had a run-in with Arthur Chandler years ago.'

'Matt's father?'

Evelyn nodded. 'Yes. He's a horrible old man, Lauren.'

'And you had a fight with him? How did that happen?'

Her mother looked down at the table and took a deep breath. 'It . . . it was just something that happened . . . something at work. What I'm trying to tell you is that he . . . he humiliated me, child.' She raised her head and her eyes flashed with cold anger. 'He thinks people like us are dirt.'

'What did you argue about?' Lauren asked curiously.

The older woman shrugged her shoulders. 'What's the difference? I . . . I wanted something better, and he said it was out of the question.'

How pale her mother was, Lauren thought, except for two spots of colour high on her cheeks. Her voice had a sudden hollow fragility to it. The anger that had carried her along for the past minutes vanished. How badly she'd handled this. She should have listened to Matt and told her mother about them calmly and rationally, instead of letting her emotions get the best of her. And whatever memory it was that her mother was reliving still pained her. She could see the anguish in the Evelyn's eyes.

'I don't know Matt's father,' Lauren said softly. 'And I'm sorry that he hurt you, but——'

'Hurt me?' Evelyn demanded furiously. 'He ruined my life!' She bit her lip. 'Well, of course that's a slight exaggeration,' she added quickly, 'but he certainly changed the course of it.'

Lauren covered her mother's hand with hers. 'I'm sure he did,' she said quietly. 'And I'm sure you really deserved the promotion he denied you. But you can't hold Matt accountable for his father's actions, can you? And he's not like that at all.'

'Like father, like son,' snapped Evelyn.

'Come on, Mother!'

'It may be a cliché, but it's true, Lauren.'

'That's absolutely ridiculous,' Lauren answered, her compassion giving way to irritation. 'Anyway, I can't imagine how anyone could carry a grudge so long.'

'I hate Arthur Chandler,' her mother said, the words delivered with staccato precision.

'I understand that, but——'

'If you understood, I wouldn't be begging for your loyalty. To think that this ... this stranger could come between us ...'

'Mother, please!'

'I suppose that's the way it is. Children grow up and parents don't have the right to expect anything.'

'That's not true,' Lauren said quickly, swallowing the anger welling within her. She knew what was happening; she recognized all the signs by now. When logic failed, guilt could always be depended upon to win the argument. But this time she wouldn't let it. She wouldn't, she wouldn't . . .

'Still, to think you'd align yourself with strangers against me . . .'

'I'd never do that,' Lauren said quickly.

'To think you'd deliberately defy me, hurt me!'

'You know I wouldn't hurt you, Mother,' Lauren said, as if by rote.

'What do you think this revelation has done to me?' her mother asked, her voice trembling.

Lauren's head drooped wearily. 'I'm sorry,' she said softly. 'I won't hurt you again. But . . .'

The tension seemed to ease from Evelyn Webster's shoulders and she slumped back in the booth.

'I might have known you'd make the right decision. Not all daughters would, you know. You can't imagine the things some of my friends go through with their children.'

God, Lauren thought in despair, her mother had misunderstood. She had to correct her . . .

'Mother, please . . .'

'You carry a child under your heart, and you suffer through its birth, and you nurture it and then . . . well, I suppose no one ever said children would return the love you give them, but you'd think they'd at least show some respect . . .' A smile lit Evelyn's face and she reached across the table and took Lauren's hand in hers. 'I'd hate to tell you how many times I've been warned that eventually you'd turn away from me, you know. "You put too much stock in that child," people say, but how could they understand how close we are, you and I?'

'Mother, I don't think you understand . . .'

'I do understand, Lauren,' the older woman insisted. She patted her daughter's hand and then got to her feet. 'There's no need to apologize. What's done is done. We all make mistakes, every now and then.' She smiled and picked up her handbag. 'Now, come on and let's see if we can't get some shopping done. You could use some new shoes, you know, and some underwear . . .'

'Mother, wait . . .'

But Evelyn was already threading her way through the restaurant. Lauren sighed and scrambled from the booth. Had her mother really misunderstood her, she wondered, or had it been more expedient to pretend she had? Had it been just an attempt at outmanoeuvering her? Well, it wasn't going to work. She wasn't about to give up Matthew Chandler. Not for anything or anybody. Not even for her mother.

CHAPTER SIX

LAUREN turned off the highway and slowed her car as she approached the marina. Ahead, the late afternoon sun was a crimson globe hung against a darkening backdrop of sky and water. She was late; Matt would have expected her hours earlier, but her mother seemed to have been revitalised by their conversation in the restaurant. She had gone back to her shopping with a vengeance, and Lauren had followed her through the crowded stores like an automaton, determined to see the day through to its end, knowing she'd won a victory even though her mother thought she'd raised a flag of surrender. And yet she'd told no lie, she reminded herself as she drove into the marina. Let sleeping dogs lie, her grandfather had always said. Well, what was wrong with that advice?

She pulled into an empty parking space near the *Lovely Lady* and shut off the engine. The kiss of the setting sun had brought a soft crimson blush to the boat's white sails and hull. Matt was on deck: she could see him doing something or other to the sails, so absorbed in his work that he hadn't even heard her old car as it chugged to a stop.

No, she thought with certainty, nothing anyone could do or say would change what she felt about him. Her feelings grew stronger each time they were together; even when they were apart, all she had to do was think of Matt and a warm glow seemed to spread through her. Did her mother really think that some unpleasant incident years before was enough to change what she felt for this man? He looked up and reached for something, and his face lit with pleasure as he saw her. Her heart soared at the realisation.

'Ahoy there!' she called, shielding her eyes with her hand as she stepped out of her car. 'Permission to come aboard?'

'Permission granted,' he said with a grin.

She smiled and reached for the hand he extended her. 'Thank you, Captain,' she said, scrambling on board.

Matt's arms closed around her and he brushed his lips lightly against her temple.

'You're welcome,' he murmured. 'Where the heck have you been? I thought you said you'd get here as soon as you could.'

'I did,' Lauren said with a sigh, leaning into his comforting embrace. 'Do you think it's easy to storm the beaches at Macy's on a sale day and emerge unscathed in less than three hours?'

'Three hours of shopping?' he chuckled in disbelief. 'You must be exhausted!'

'Exhausted, starved, achey ... it was a full-scale assault on the sales racks, Captain.'

Matt dropped a light kiss on her forehead. 'Can you hold on for just a little while longer? This only needs another five minutes and then I'll shower and change and take you out to dinner so you can recoup your strength.'

Lauren smiled and stepped from of his embrace. 'Sure. What are you doing, anyway?'

'Mending this sail,' he said, picking up a heavy needle and stabbing it through the fabric. He worked in silence for a couple of minutes while she watched, then he glanced up and smiled. 'Why so quiet, sweetheart?'

'I'm just tired, I guess. It was a long day.'

'I thought shopping was supposed to revitalise the female of the species,' he said teasingly. The smile faded from his face and his eyes met hers. 'You didn't have a very good day, did you?'

She sighed and smiled weakly. 'No,' she admitted. 'Not really. It's as if my mother and I belong to the argument of the day club.'

'You quarrelled, you mean.'

She nodded. 'I started to tell her that you and I have been seeing each other,' she said slowly, running her hand along the teak railing. 'I didn't get very far. I suppose I should have picked a better time ... but it just slipped out.'

'I get the feeling she was less than thrilled,' said Matt with forced lightness.

'An understatement if ever I heard one, Captain,' Lauren said with a sigh. 'You are definitely not one of her favourite people.'

He shook his head and jabbed the needle into the fabric again. 'I told you it's time I talked to her, Lauren. Let her tell me, to my face, what she has against me.'

'She thinks you're out to break my heart and toss the pieces overboard.'

'That can't be the reason ...'

Lauren sighed again and leaned back against the railing. 'No,' she admitted after a few seconds silence, 'there's more than that. She had some kind of run-in with your father.'

With a sudden vicious thrust, Matt jabbed the needle into the sail. 'When the hell did that happen?' he demanded angrily, swinging around to her. 'If that old man interfered in my life again ... He knows I'm not going to tolerate any more nonsense!'

'No, no—you don't understand,' she said quickly, putting her hand on his arm. She could feel the muscle tensing beneath her fingers. 'This happened years ago—before I was born, for God's sake. It had something to do with a promotion or something. Whatever it was, she's never forgotten it.'

Matt's eyebrows arched quizzically. 'Let me be sure I've got this right,' he said slowly, putting his hands on his hips. 'Your mother hates me because of something my father did more than twenty years ago?' Lauren nodded in mute acknowledgement. 'Wow,' he said softly. 'The lady really knows how to hold a grudge, doesn't she?'

'I know it sounds crazy ... She didn't go into details, but apparently she asked your father for a better job and he turned her down. I'm certain she thinks that would have made all the difference in her life, and ...' She moved her shoulders in an apologetic half-shrug. 'Look, I think she's dotty, too, if you want to know the truth. But there isn't anything I can do about it.'

Matt wiped his hands on his cut-down denims and pulled the needle through the sailcloth.

'You can let me tell her that keeping people apart because their parents don't like each other went out with the Montagues and Capulets,' he muttered, clipping the heavy thread and setting the needle aside.

Lauren smiled despite herself. 'Leave that to me,' she said gently. 'I doubt if she'd listen to you just yet.'

He smiled and his eyes met hers. 'Did you at least tell her I don't want to break your heart?' he asked softly. 'Does she know that I just want to steal it?'

'She warned me about sailors when I was a little

girl,' Lauren teased. 'She said a girl couldn't trust them!'

Matt grinned and pulled her into his arms. 'Well, she was right about that, at least,' he laughed. Lauren smiled up at him and his arms tightened around her. 'I wish to hell your mother would listen to reason,' he murmured. 'She's going to have to accept me, sooner or later. I'm not going to go away or disappear or change my mind about you . . .'

'Are you sure of that, Captain?'

His answer was to cover her mouth with his in a kiss that told her everything she had ever wanted to know. The sweetness of his lips, the warmth of his hands as they moved slowly across her back, seemed to free the knowledge she had been holding within herself for days.

I love you, she thought suddenly, the words so sharply defined in her mind that, for a split second, she thought she'd said them aloud. They were the same words Matt had whispered to her a week before, but she'd been too stunned to respond. Now she realised she'd been waiting days for a chance to tell him how she felt, but the simple phrase was hard to voice. She buried her face in the curve of his shoulder, wishing for the courage to say it aloud.

'If you want dinner, you have ten seconds to move away from me,' he whispered suddenly. 'Otherwise I'm going to snatch you up in my arms, carry you across the deck, and . . .'

'You can't get out of our date that easily,' laughed Lauren, pushing him gently from her. 'Besides, I'm starved. If I don't eat soon, I'm going to do a very maidenlike swoon right here on deck!'

Matt grinned as he started towards the companionway. 'No, there's no point to that. It would be wasted on me. You'd only be doing that in hopes I'd take advantage of you!'

'Oh, what conceit you harbour, Captain,' she laughed. 'I'd hoped no such thing!'

He chuckled and started below deck. 'That's good to hear,' he called over his shoulder, 'because I wouldn't touch a swooning female. The woman I take advantage of has to be willing to take advantage of me in return. I'm a believer in equal opportunity . . .'

He ducked as Lauren tossed a cushion at his retreating back. She smiled and settled against the railing to wait for him.

The evening breeze ruffled the water gently, carrying with it a faint, mysterious scent of distant places. The orange halo of the disappearing sun was dusting the placid bay when Matt reappeared on deck, dressed in grey flannel slacks, blue blazer, and white turtleneck sweater. His dark hair was still damp from the shower.

'You look beautiful,' Lauren said solemnly. 'I thought I'm supposed to be the one who looks that way.'

He grinned and put his arm around her shoulders. 'Stop fishing for compliments, you shameless woman. You look gorgeous and you know it.'

'I am not fishing,' she said happily, smiling up at him. 'But you can tell me more, if you like.'

'You'd better stop snuggling up to me that way,' he warned, 'or I'm going to deprive San Francisco of the chance to see how beautiful you are tonight. That was a double compliment,' he added helpfully, 'just in case you're keeping score. I managed to get in something about your sex appeal as well as your looks.' He laughed as Lauren made a face and punched his arm.

Night had fallen by the time Matt's Corvette purred towards the heart of the city. All around them, the hills that made up San Francisco blazed with light. They parked on a street so steep that they laughed as they stumbled out of the car and struggled uphill towards the Fairmont Hotel. An elevator took them to the hotel's rooftop cocktail lounge, and Lauren stared out at the spectacular sprawl of the city beneath them with unabashed delight.

'Do I look like a tourist?' she asked. 'Well, I don't care if I do,' she added, answering her own question with defiance. 'I never knew the view was so wonderful from up here.' Her eyes shone with pleasure as she turned from the enormous window and smiled at Matt. 'Did I really hear you order Moët & Chandon champagne?' she demanded. 'Tell me I imagined that, please.'

He shook his head and grinned. 'Just don't tell anybody. If you do, I promise I'll deny everything.' He paused as their waiter appeared at their tableside with the chilled bottle of wine. The bottle opened with an appropriately muffled sound, and Matt nodded approvingly after taking the first necessary sip. 'Just taste it,' he advised, after the man had moved away, 'and you'll know why I ordered it.'

Lauren smiled. 'Don't ever admit it to a French vintner,' she said, 'but I'm not sure we'll ever be able to match their champagne.' She sipped the delicate, sparkling liquid and then put her glass down on the table. 'Are we celebrating something tonight?'

Matt's eyes met hers. 'Yes, I think we are,' he answered. 'We're celebrating the fact that, for better or worse, your mother knows about us.'

Lauren's face fell and she set her glass down before her. 'Then there really isn't anything to celebrate, is there?'

'Indeed there is,' Matt said quickly, covering her hand with his. 'She ordered you not to see me any more, didn't she?'

'How did you know that?'

He smiled. 'Women don't have a monopoly on intuition, Lauren.'

'Yes, she did,' she admitted.

'And here you are anyway,' he said, taking her hand in his.

Her eyes met his with unflinching directness. 'Here I am anyway,' she repeated clearly.

'You see?' he murmured softly, lifting her hand to his mouth. 'I told you we had something to celebrate. She knows about us, sweetheart, she doesn't approve, and yet here you are.'

Lauren shook her head. 'And that's something to celebrate? I don't understand . . .'

Matt leaned towards her and ran his finger along her jaw. 'I know how important she is to you, Lauren. I know how responsible you feel for her.' He smiled and touched his finger to her lips. 'I guess what I'm trying to say is that I get the idea I'm important to you—or you wouldn't be willing to stand up to her the way you have.'

She could feel herself blushing. 'What was it you said about yourself when we first met? That you were modest and humble?'

'I'm not joking this time, Lauren. Unless I've made a judgement I shouldn't . . .'

'No, you haven't,' she admitted in a whisper.

He smiled. 'I didn't think so.'

'Matt . . .'

'That's one reason to celebrate,' he said, lifting his glass and touching it to hers. 'And I'm betting we'll find others if we try. Remember, the night isn't over yet.'

An hour later, with only half the champagne finished, they traded the elegance of the Fairmont for the narrow, crowded streets of Chinatown, searching for a restaurant Matt swore he remembered from his childhood, settling at last for a half-empty, tiny old place perched like a tree house at the top of a creaking flight of wooden steps. A smiling old woman bowed them into the exotic confines of a private booth, screened from the curious by a beaded curtain, and Lauren listened in baffled amazement as Matt rattled off a string of musical phrases in Chinese.

'What was that?' she asked as soon as the old woman had bowed and shuffled off.

'Dinner for two, I hope,' he laughed. 'I went to school with some guy from Shanghai. Thanks to him, I know enough to get from soup to dessert.'

But it wasn't all he knew, Lauren thought two hours later, as Matt and the old woman bowed to each other and parted. He'd managed some sort of conversation each time she'd reappeared at their booth, and when they left, she whispered a final something, glanced at Lauren, and giggled.

'What was that all about?' Lauren demanded as she made her way carefully down the steep steps. 'Was she making fun of the way I used my chopsticks?'

Matt laughed and took her hand as she reached the bottom of the stairs. 'I don't know if I should tell you . . .'

'I knew it! She was making fun of me—It isn't

easy to use chopsticks the very first time, you know. And especially when you're eating dumplings!'

'She said she'd been watching your face when you looked at me.'

'Watching me drop the dumplings, you mean.'

'She said see watched your eyes, especially.'

'I dropped the crab claws, too, but . . .'

Matt took her other hand and drew her slowly towards him. 'She prides herself on having a kind of sixth sense,' he said softly. 'She told me that she knows you haven't said so yet, but that you're in love with me.'

His words were light and bantering, but there was a tenseness underlying them, and his eyes seemed to be searching her soul.

'She didn't say that . . .' Lauren said hesitantly.

'She did,' he insisted. 'I told her that might have been important news to me earlier tonight, but that it wasn't any more.'

Lauren looked at him warily. 'Why not?' she asked, despite herself.

'Because of the way you used your chopsticks,' he said patiently. 'After all, what man would be interested in loving a woman who drops dumplings all over herself?'

She could see the faint smile on his face, a smile that couldn't change the fact that his hands had tightened on hers. She wanted to move closer to him and kiss the place where the dark hair curled behind his ear, or the slightly upturned corner of his mouth, but instead she took a deep breath and spoke over the loud, insistent hammering of her heart.

'You are a terrible person,' she said in a low, clear voice, 'and you have a cruel sense of humour, and in spite of all that, I love you with all my heart.'

A tremor ran through her when she saw the effect her words had on him. His smile widened and his eyes darkened and softened with pleasure.

'Are you sure?' he whispered.

She nodded her head. 'Absolutely certain,' she whispered, and he pulled her into his arms and held her tightly against his chest. 'I love you, Matt.' A smile tugged at the corners of her mouth. 'I just wish I'd been the first one to tell you,' she added, laughing softly.

'You were,' he admitted with a grin. 'You were right about the old lady. All she told me was not to give up on you just because you were clumsy.'

'You really are terrible,' Lauren repeated with mock indignation. 'What on earth am I going to do with you?'

He chuckled softly. 'I thought you'd never ask!'

They stepped hurriedly apart as the door opened and a group of tourists clattered up the stairs towards the restaurant. The door on the upper landing slammed shut, and Matt cleared his throat.

'It's decision time,' he said softly.

She nodded her head, knowing at once precisely what he meant. The air between them felt charged with electricity.

'We can drive up to Twin Peaks and look at the city . . .'

'I've seen the city,' Lauren said carefully.

'Or we can go to the Top of the Mark for an after-dinner drink . . .'

'I'm not much for after-dinner drinks.'

His eyes were the colour of smoke as he moved closer to her. 'I could take you home . . .'

'It's much too early for that,' she said quickly.

'Well, there's only one other choice, then. We can

drive back to the *Lovely Lady* and I'll teach you about moonlight navigation.'

Lauren took a deep breath and raised her eyes to his. 'I thought you'd never ask!'

The marina was deserted and quiet, the stillness broken only by the rhythmic lap of the water against the dock. Lauren's high heels sounded unnaturally loud; she slipped her shoes from her feet and carried them in her hand as Matt offered her his outstretched hand and helped her aboard the boat. The moon was high and full as it rode the black sky; the cool, creamy glow it cast on the water was shattered into tiny shards of white light by wavelets in their ceaseless quest for the shore.

She took his hand and moved into his open arms without hesitation, her eyes closing as his mouth brushed against hers. They had been quiet during the ride back to the marina, listening to the soft strains of a Rachmaninoff piano concerto on the radio. Lauren's hand had been clasped tightly in Matt's; he would not relinquish it even when he had to change gear. Her thoughts had been clear and certain. She wanted him to make love to her, and she wanted to make love to him: it was all one and the same, and there were no more questions or doubts. She'd glanced at him once or twice, wondering if it was necessary to tell him that, but now, in his arms, she knew that he understood everything.

She wound her arms around his neck and buried her face against his throat. She could feel his pulse surging strongly beneath her lips, and exulted to know that it was racing like hers. He rubbed his cheek against hers and the faint stubble of his beard was like a kiss against her skin. Gently, his hand clasped her chin and he raised her face to his. 'Beautiful Lauren,' he murmured softly, as if her name were a benediction, and then he kissed her. His mouth was so warm, she thought, so sweet—and then it was impossible to think of anything. She could only feel and taste his lips as his kisses told her everything she had wanted to hear.

'Lauren,' he whispered, 'Lauren,' and she sighed as she heard the night wind pick up the soft cry and carry it aloft. His hands slid to her waist and then up to cup her breasts. He whispered her name again, or was it she whispering his? It was impossible to tell; she was spinning, spinning . . . and then she was in his arms, clinging tightly to his neck, and he was striding rapidly to the companionway.

The darkness below deck was almost complete. The cabin, blacker than the night sky, was pierced only by a ray of moonlight that burnished the bunk with silvery luminescence. Gently, Matt lowered her to the bunk. She reached for him, speaking his name as he drew away, and then he was in her arms again, kneeling beside her, and when her hands touched him, she knew he'd taken off his jacket. She could feel the hard ridges of muscle under his soft cotton shirt, and her fingers played over his shoulders and down his back as he gathered her to him.

Her lips parted willingly under the demanding pressure of his, and she tangled her fingers in the silky, curling hair at the nape of his neck. Their bodies strained together, mouth to mouth, but it wasn't enough for Lauren. She wanted to be closer to this man she loved, to become part of him, to consume him and be consumed by him. She moved against him with an intuitive sensuality born of need and he groaned softly.

'I love you, Lauren,' he murmured hoarsely.

In the velvet darkness, her fingers played across his face. He caught her hand and brought it to his mouth.

'Make love to me, Matt,' she whispered. 'Make love to me . . .'

He opened the zipper that ran down the back of her dress, and she shrugged impatiently as the fabric slid silkily from her shoulders. The night air was cool against her skin, but Matt's hands were warm and his mouth searing as it caressed her. Her head fell back, exposing her throat to his exploring kisses, and his lips left a heated, exciting trail from the soft hollow where her pulse beat wildly to the curving softness of her breast. He kissed the swelling curve rising above her silk camisole, and then his lips and teeth teased the heated flesh awaiting him beneath the thin covering. Lauren gasped at the sensation. Suddenly, even the sheer fabric that separated them was too much, and she moved impatiently within his embrace.'

'Don't be afraid,' he murmured softly, his lips inches from hers. 'I won't hurt you, darling.'

'I'm not afraid,' she whispered shamelessly. 'I just want to feel you against me, Matt . . . your mouth, your hands, your body . . .'

He made a sound deep in his throat, and then the delicate piece of silk was gone, flung aside. She heard the whisper of fabric as his shirt followed after, and then she was in his arms, her breasts pressed against the hard, muscled wonder of his chest, her hands tangled in the thick darkness of his hair. He stirred against her, cradling her in his arms as he stretched out next to her on the bunk, and her lips brushed against his throat. How warm his skin was, she thought with a stir of pleasure. She traced a line of kisses to the curve of his shoulder and down his chest, revelling in the taste of him, a blend of sun and sea and something more, something that was Matt. Her kisses and her increasingly bold exploratory touches pleased him, she knew; she could hear his sharp intake of breath and the soft, encouraging sounds he made as she touched him.

'I love you, Matt,' she whispered, although the words seemed so inadequate for the enormity of what she felt. 'I love you . . .

His mouth was everywhere, a honeyed caress on her lips, her throat, her breasts, creating sensations within her that were beyond anything she had ever dreamed possible. Suddenly, the remaining clothing that separated them was a barrier, and her fingers and his eased her dress from her body. Lauren gazed up at Matt as he bent over her. In the virginal white light of the high-riding moon, she could see the mingling of love and desire in his eyes, and she knew it was a reflection of what he must see in hers. She lifted her arms, welcoming him to her, knowing that she burned with a fire only his body could quench.

And when finally his gentle, exciting touch turned to a possessive demand from which there could be no turning back, the world was reduced to nothing but the boat gently rocking beneath them and the endless, infinite sea.

CHAPTER SEVEN

LAUREN peered forward and scanned the letter in her typewriter. Had she really spelled Chardonnay wrongly, not just once but twice in the same paragraph? Yes, she certainly had, and she'd left a word out, right at the end.

'Damn!'

The softly uttered oath exploded from her before she could stop it, and an embarrassed blush rose to her cheeks as her eyes met those of the young woman working at the next desk.

'Sorry,' she apologised quickly. 'I just can't believe how badly I've botched this letter.'

The other woman smiled sympathetically. 'One of those days, huh?'

Lauren sighed as she ripped the offending letter from her typewriter and tossed it aside.

'One of those weeks,' she said with a rueful smile. 'I haven't done one thing right.' She swallowed the rest of her words as she saw her supervisor approaching. The stern expression on the woman's face was not reassuring.

'Lauren, would you step outside for a minute, please?' Mrs Lane asked crisply.

Well, Lauren thought glumly, as she followed her to the door, there would be no delighted comments about her work, not this time. You could hide a couple of off-days, but not a whole week of them. Her fingers couldn't seem to find the right keys on the typewriter and even when they did, they moved

with a slow, clumsy rhythm that resulted in a
growing stack of crumpled letters lying discarded in
the waste basket.

And what excuse could she possibly offer? That
she was in love? Love was supposed to put wings on
your feet, not lead boots, although, as she'd learned
these past few days, it could seem as much a burden
as a joy when you found yourself caught between the
only two people you cared for. Her mother's refusal
even to hear Matt's name, and Matt's increasing
impatience with keeping their relationship secret,
was exacting a high price on her emotions. Not that
her supervisor would accept that as an excuse, even
if she could tell her any of it.

'Your work has been less than satisfactory this
week, Lauren,' Sunny Lane said, closing the door
behind her.

Well, that was to the point, Lauren thought. Her
response would be the same.

'I know it, Mrs Lane. All I can say is that I'm
aware of it, and I'm sorry . . .'

'So am I, Lauren. I'd intended to speak to you
about your performance. But now . . .' She shook her
head and sighed. 'Believe me, if I had anyone else,
I'd never consider offering you this opportunity.'

The woman's solemnly delivered comments had
sounded like the preface to being told she was fired;
it took a couple of seconds to shift mental gears and
realise she was talking about some sort of upgrading
instead.

'I don't understand,' Lauren said slowly. 'What
opportunity?'

'I've just had a call from upstairs. Mr Chandler's
secretary is out sick again and they need you. To
operate the word processor, Lauren,' the woman

added impatiently when Lauren looked blank. 'Believe me, if it weren't for the fact that I have no one else who can operate that machine, I wouldn't send you. Not this time. Your work . . .'

'Has been below par—yes, I know,' Lauren said quickly, trying her best to sound humble and penitent although the thought of being transferred to Matt's office for the day made her want to grab her supervisor by the shoulders and kiss her. 'I'll do better, Mrs Lane.'

The woman's stern expression softened. 'I certainly hope so, Lauren. After all, this assignment is important. I wouldn't want you to disappoint Mr Chandler.'

'I'll try not to,' Lauren said carefully, trying desperately not to smile as she thought of all the ways such an innocent comment might be interpreted. 'I'll do my best.'

Matt probably didn't know she'd been assigned to him, she thought as she hurried down the hall to his office minutes later. Finding a replacement for an absent secretary was an automatic procedure. She smiled to herself as she thought of how pleased he'd be when he saw her.

The door to the reception area of his office was ajar, but the room was empty. Lauren dropped her things on the desk near the word processor and then glanced at the closed door to his private office. She ran her hands through her hair, fluffing it up from her shoulders, and pushed her glasses further up her nose. Why in heaven's name hadn't she worn her contact lenses today, she thought with sudden illogical irritation, then she took a deep breath and knocked at his door.

There was no answer, and she frowned and

knocked again. There was still no answer. Maybe he
wasn't in yet . . . after all, it was barely mid-morning.
No, he was always at his desk by nine unless he was
out in the vineyards or off on an appointment. He'd
said something about meeting a vintner in San José,
she remembered, but was it today or tomorrow? If it
were today, she thought with a deadening rush of
disappointment, she might spend the entire day
finishing the work she'd seen stacked next to the
word processor without even seeing him.

But if he was in the washroom, he wouldn't have
heard her knock, especially if he'd been out in the
vineyards and he'd decided to shower.

She pushed open the door and went into his office.
It was empty, and the door to the washroom was ajar.
Both rooms were empty. She felt a sharp stab of
disappointment. He was probably in San José.

Suddenly the door slammed shut behind her. The
unexpected sound was like a gunshot in the quiet
room. Lauren gasped and started to turn, but a
strong arm enfolded her and a hand covered her
eyes.

'A kiss, or your life is forfeit, my proud beauty,' a
familiar voice growled in her ear.

'Matt, you crazy fool, let go of me!' she demanded
in a whisper. 'Someone might come in . . .'

In answer, he turned her to face him and gave her
a lazy smile. 'That's one of the privileges of rank,
sweetheart. No one dares open the closed door to the
inner sanctum without knocking.' He kissed the tip
of her nose. 'Good morning, Miss Webster. How do
you like your new assignment?'

'You mean you knew?'

'Knew?' He laughed wickedly. 'I told Personnel to
have you sent up here. They were going to send me

some creaking veteran from the file room, but I reminded them that I had a word processor, and that we had an employee in the secretarial pool who was qualified to operate it.'

She laughed softly. 'Sounds good to me, boss, although I don't know how qualified you'll think I am by the end of the day. I've made a million mistakes . . .'

His arms tightened around her. 'Can you keep a secret?'

'A secret?' she repeated.

'A top priority secret,' Matt said solemnly. 'You don't have to worry about making mistakes. The word processor's broken. It has been since yesterday.'

It was impossible not to return his grin, even though she tried valiantly to look disapproving.

'You're going to make it awfully hard for me to do as my supervisor asked, Mr Chandler,' she said archly.

'Mrs Lane?'

Lauren fluttered her lashes in a deliberate parody of girlish innocence and nodded her head.

'Yes, sir, Mr Chandler. She said she hoped I wouldn't disappoint you.'

Matt burst into laughter and hugged her tightly. 'I hope you told her not to worry about it.'

'I told her I'd do my best,' said Lauren with a giggle. She shook her head and leaned back against the comforting circle of his arms. 'I couldn't believe it when she told me I was being sent to your office.'

'We'll have to thank my secretary. The poor woman's developed some sort of back problem. She called me this morning and said she's going to have to stay home for a couple of weeks.'

'Weeks?' Lauren repeated.

He nodded solemnly. 'At least. Maybe even a month.'

'That's awful,' Lauren answered, struggling to look as if it were indeed awful and not succeeding very well. 'I'm so sorry she's ill.'

'I am too,' he said, and then a faint smile played across his mouth. 'It's terrible to get such pleasure out of someone else's misfortune, isn't it?'

'Do you really mean to tell me we're going to spend each day together for the next ...' Suddenly, a shadow darkened her eyes and she shook her head. 'I don't know ...' she said slowly, catching her bottom lip between her teeth. 'I mean, it would be okay for a day or two, but weeks ...'

'You don't have to worry about Mrs Lane. I'll have Personnel notify her that you've been reassigned.'

'I was thinking of my mother ... She'll have a fit.'

'Lauren,' Matt said carefully, 'I think this has gone just about as far as it can. You must tell her about us.'

'I will, I promise. I just need a little more time ...'

He shook his head and dropped his arms to his sides. 'You know, when I was a kid, this might have been terrific. Dating a girl on the sly, sneaking around in the shadows ... but I'm not a kid any more, and neither are you. I love you, Lauren. I don't want to hide that.'

'Matt, please be patient ...'

'I have been,' he said, walking to the window. 'I've been more than patient, haven't I? I offered to face her ... but you said no. You said it would be best if you told her yourself.'

'And it will be, believe me,' Lauren insisted. 'Try and understand, Matt. I'm all she has. She ... she's easily hurt, you see. She's sure she knows what's best for me, and when I disagree—well, she takes it personally. She thinks it means I'm rejecting her.'

Matt shook his head. 'Come on,' he said roughly, turning his back on the fields of ripening grapes visible through the window. 'Don't hide behind armchair psychoanalysis.'

She held her hands out to him imploringly. 'I'm not . . .'

'Maybe you just aren't sure about us?'

She flinched as if someone had struck her. 'Is that why I haven't seen anyone but you since the day we met?' she demanded. 'Is that why I want to spend every second with you? Is that why I've been lying to my mother?' Her voice broke and she turned away just as Matt's arms closed tightly around her.

'I'm sorry, darling,' he whispered, turning her around in his embrace. 'I didn't mean that. It's just that I feel so goddamned frustrated sometimes. I get this crazy urge to drive to your house at least once a night. I mean, I want to go right to the door and ring the bell, or call you on the phone!' He grinned wistfully. 'Exotic, huh?'

'Matt, we've been all through this . . .'

'Damn right we have,' he said quickly, the impatient tone returning to his voice. 'And each and every time, you tell me to be patient.'

'Do you think I like this any more than you do?' Lauren demanded, moving out of his arms. 'I'm trying to work it out, Matt. I want her to like you.'

'Dammit, she doesn't have to like me!' he exploded. 'I'm not out to win a popularity contest, Lauren. All I want to do is step out of the shadows.' His eyes scanned her face and then he sighed and shook his head. 'Look, sweetheart, I admit things

would be easier if she approved, but you're of age.
You have the right to make your own decisions. You
can't go on feeling guilty for wanting to live your own
life.'

'It isn't that,' she protested, shaking her head. 'I
just keep hoping she'll change her mind about you.'

Matt held out his hand. 'Tell me how that can
happen if she refuses to see me,' he asked reasonably.

'I don't know,' she admitted with an unhappy
sigh. 'I'll figure something out.'

He drew her to him and slipped his arms around
her. 'Life isn't always what we want it to be, Lauren,'
he said softly. 'Sometimes it's impossible to have
fairy-tale endings.'

'I don't want fairy-tale endings, Matt. I simply
want the two people who matter most to me to like
each other. Is that so much to ask?'

'What happens if they don't?' he asked quietly.

Lauren shook her head. 'Don't say that,' she said
quickly. 'That won't happen.'

Matt tilted her face up to his. 'What if it does?' he
insisted, his eyes searching hers. 'Are you prepared
to make a choice if you have to?'

'Matt, for God's sake—that isn't going to happen.
My mother will change her mind, you'll see. She has
to . . .'

He sighed and drew her head to his chest. 'I hope
so, for your sake, Lauren. But I think you ought to at
least consider the possibility. I mean, it doesn't seem
likely she's going to change her mind suddenly about
me even though her attitude doesn't make a damned
bit of sense.'

'It makes sense to her, Matt,' Lauren said quickly.
She shook her head as she realised how defensive her
answer sounded. 'Let's not quarrel about her,

please,' she said, painfully aware of what Matt had just said about making choices. 'I just need some time . . .'

'What you need is to cut the cord, sweetheart,' said Matt, tilting her face up to his again. 'Don't you see what a hold she has on you?'

She touched his face with her hand. 'You have a hold on me,' she said in a quavering whisper. 'I love you, Matt.'

The tension left his face and he smiled. 'Do you, Miss Webster?'

'Absolutely, Mr Chandler.'

He chuckled softly. 'How much do you love me?' he asked wickedly.

'More than a magnum of Lafite Rothschild . . . a vintage year, of course.'

'That's pretty convincing,' Matt agreed solemnly. 'But it's not enough.'

'Okay, then,' she said thoughtfully, cocking her head to the side, 'I love you more than . . . more than . . . don't do that,' she whispered as he began to kiss her neck. 'Matt, I can't think . . .'

'You're beginning to convince me,' he murmured as a tremor ran through her. 'But I still have some doubts . . .'

'You couldn't possibly,' she whispered huskily. 'Not now.'

'I do, though. Let me just lock this door . . .'

'You wouldn't!' she protested in horror. His low chuckle was so deliberate that she needed no other answer. 'Absolutely not,' she said, trying unsuccessfully to free herself from his embrace. 'I couldn't . . . we couldn't . . .'

'We certainly could!' he laughed.

'We have work to do. And sooner or later,

somebody is going to come to the door.'

'That's what locks are for, Lauren.'

Suddenly, as if by design, there was a knock at the door. Lauren paled and struggled to free herself.

'Yes? Who's there?' Matt asked calmly, ignoring her desperate efforts to move away from his encircling arms.

'Matt . . . let go of me!' she whispered frantically, while a voice outside the door explained that the month's sales figures had arrived.

'Just leave them on my secretary's desk,' called Matt, holding Lauren even more closely. 'I'm rather busy at the moment.'

Lauren closed her eyes in despair. 'If we don't open this door in thirty seconds, this building will buzz with rumours!'

'Will it?' Matt asked innocently. 'Yes, I guess it will. Well, I'm willing to open the door—but first you have to promise you'll have lunch with me!'

'Is that all you want?' Lauren asked suspiciously.

'Would you prefer something more?' he laughed.

'You're terrible,' she said, blushing furiously. 'I'd love to have lunch with you.'

'On board the boat,' he added with a smile.

'Matt, we can't . . . we're supposed to be working!'

His smile broadened into a grin and he chuckled softly. 'We will be,' he assured her solemnly. 'I guarantee it.'

'I don't underst——' A pink blush replaced Lauren's puzzled frown and she shook her head. 'You really are terrible,' she whispered happily. 'But who am I to argue with my employer?'

CHAPTER EIGHT

AUTUMN comes slowly to the Napa Valley. Warmed by the nearby Pacific Ocean, the fertile land clings to summer until late in September, when the night breeze that sighs through the dark green grape leaves begins to carry a hint of coolness, and the fruit itself hangs heavy and sweet on the vines, ready for harvest.

Lauren drove slowly along a narrow back road that wound between fields of ripening grapes. She was in no rush to get home. In fact, the trip took longer this way, but she needed time to make the transition from being Matt's lover to being Evelyn Webster's daughter. Taking the long way back to San Jacinto gave her an extra few minutes in which to adjust. It was like a decompression chamber, she thought with a faint smile, a place in which to maintain a balance between the two differing realities of her life.

She had been working with Matt for several weeks, and it still seemed like a small miracle to awaken each morning and look forward to spending an entire day with him. Her mother had complained, of course, but Lauren had simply pointed out that she was the only person able to operate Matt's word processor until his secretary returned.

Nothing could spoil the pleasure of the hours she and Matt shared. And Lauren had learned more about growing grapes and making wine than she had in all the courses she'd taken or textbooks she'd read.

Matt involved himself in every part of the wine-making progress, from nursing along the first green shoots in the vineyards to inspecting the bottles of wine as they were transferred on to trucks from the loading dock. Today was Saturday, but they'd spent it tramping through rows of Cabernet Sauvignon grapes ripening under the hot sun.

'You shouldn't work today,' her mother had said early that morning, 'not after being sick during the night. He has a nerve anyway, asking you to work at the weekend.'

'I feel fine, Mother. It was probably just something I ate. And I won't have to work all day. It'll just be for a few hours.'

And that had turned out to be the absolute truth, Lauren thought, smiling to herself. They had worked during the cool morning hours and then, as the sun rose higher, they had walked slowly, hand in hand, along a ridge above the vineyards. And then there had been the wonderful hour spent in each other's arms in the old wine shed . . .

A delicious shudder went through her. Oh, how she loved Matt! He was everything she'd ever wanted in a man. He was handsome and good and kind and . . . and he had the patience of Job, she thought with a sigh. Sometimes she was afraid that he was disappointed in her. Perhaps disappointed was too strong a word, she thought as she merged into the sparse Saturday afternoon traffic heading south towards San Jacinto. But she knew he was convinced she let her mother manipulate her. It wasn't true, of course; she knew all her mother's tricks by now and how to ignore them. It was just that she'd trapped herself in a web of lies, and it was hard to break free of that kind of entanglement. But the time had finally come; Matt had seen to that an hour earlier.

'I just want to check my Chardonnay,' he'd said, pulling up next to the shed where the first bottles of the *premier cru*, estate-bottled white wine were stored. 'Okay with you?'

'Sure,' she answered, suppressing a smile at how he'd described the wine as his. She blinked in the sudden darkness of the building and shivered as the cool air touched her sun-heated skin. A roiling wave of nausea clutched at her throat for a second and then subsided.

'Are you okay? Lauren?'

She nodded her head. 'Yes, I'm fine. Really, Matt—I'm okay.' She smiled reassuringly. 'That's what happens when you work the peasants too hard under the burning sun, Mr Chandler.'

Matt laughed. 'Wrong, Miss Webster. That's what happens when you're kind enough to bring the peasants into the shade. Next time, I'll leave you in the car to sweat.'

'I'm a lady peasant,' she said primly. 'I don't sweat, I perspire.'

'Well, sit down on that stool and dry off,' he laughed. 'This will only take a few minutes.'

The wine bottles lay angled in old wooden racks before them, glinting green in the murky shadows. Matt ran his hand over one and smiled.

'It's ready—or maybe I should say it's as ready as I can make it.'

'You really are modest and humble, aren't you?' Lauren teased. 'You know it's terrific wine, Matt. Your only problem is going to be finding wall space for all the awards you're going to get.'

He reached out and ruffled her hair. 'You're good for my ego, sweetheart,' he said with a grin. 'I just hope some of those accolades come from my father. If not . . .' He shrugged and let out a sigh. 'Well, we'll deal with that when the time comes.'

'If the time comes,' Lauren said quickly. 'Anyway, what's the worst that can happen? Surely he knows you can never predict how a wine will be received?'

Matt laughed and put his arm around her shoulders. 'You're an innocent, sweetheart. I told you how he fought me on this; I think Chandler's future is in making limited, fine wines, and he thinks it's a foolish risk when we can go on producing our old mass market standbys. If my Chardonnay doesn't get rave reviews and sales, he and I will go toe to toe on the future of the winery.'

'But you have as much to say about things as he does, don't you? Your mother left you her half . . .'

'I wish to hell it were that simple. Sure, we're equal partners on paper, but in reality he never lets me forget that he owned Chandler's long before I was born. And he's right, of course. When you get down to the bottom line, it really belongs to him.'

'But he defers to your decisions. You're responsible for the operation of the winery, Matt. No one even sees him . . .'

Matt hugged her lightly and smiled. 'The old man's "retirement", you mean. Believe me, at the end of damned near every day, I have to describe each decision I made, each action I took . . . We see Chandler's differently. To him, it's a faceless, profitable business. To me . . . I love the place, Lauren. I want it to prosper as much as he does, but . . .'

Lauren slipped her arm around his waist. 'You don't have to explain. My grandfather felt the same way. I can still remember the way he talked about the land he used to own, describing it as if it were alive, and then my mother would ask how big a crop it had produced.'

Matt's arm tightened around her. 'I'm not just a dreamer, and he knows it. Fine wines may not produce a profit for us for a while, but I'm certain they will eventually. If he doesn't want to back them, we're going to have an argument to end them all.'

'Even if that happened, you'd work it out.'

He sighed and shrugged his shoulders. 'Who knows, Lauren? We've disagreed more and more since he retired; I suppose he feels as if I'm pushing him aside and bringing in my own ideas. All I know is that one of these days we're going to face off on something irreconcilable, and either he'll back down or I'll end up walking away from Chandler's.'

'Oh, Matt, you could never do that!'

He shrugged again. 'Maybe you're right. I can no more picture walking out on this place . . . I've put my blood and sweat into it ever since I was a kid. Still, there are some things a man can't let pass. Well, let's hope it never comes to that.'

Lauren looked at his tense face. 'Nobody will be able to let your Chardonnay pass,' she said lightly. 'The dealers will be lining up to order it.'

He laughed, and she could almost see the strain easing from his taut shoulders.

'I didn't know you could predict the future, Miss Webster.'

'I'm a fortune-teller, Mr Chandler,' she said with a grin. 'Haven't I ever shown you my tarot cards?'

'Take them with you to the Harvest Dance tonight. You can liven up the evening, if things get dull.'

'Lord, don't tempt me,' she sighed. 'I mean, can

you just picture the reaction I'd get if I went to the Club dressed as a gypsy, shuffling a deck of cards?' She giggled and buried her face against Matt's chest. 'It would almost be worth it just to see Mrs Harrow's face!'

'How about seeing my face?' said Matt, tilting her chin up. 'Without the gypsy fortune-teller outfit or the cards, of course,' he added with a smile.

'Matt, I told you the other day—I'm not going. You know that.'

'Yes, but . . . well, according to my father, I have to show up.'

'I thought he was out of town.'

'He is. He's in Los Angeles, working out some preliminary ideas with an advertising agency for a new ad campaign. That's how "retired" he is,' Matt added with a wry smile. 'Anyway, he phoned me last night to remind me that it's traditional that new wines be introduced at the Club the night of the dance. I think the whole thing is foolish, but I don't want to do anything to rock the boat. So far, all he's said about the Chardonnay is that it isn't bad.'

'Isn't bad?' Lauren repeated indignantly, leaning back against his encircling arms and staring at him. It's wonderful!'

'Well, the fact that he wants to have it served tonight is a pretty good sign, sweetheart. He says he's going to try to be there, too. He has some sort of meeting to attend, but he's arranged for a charter flight out of L.A. this evening. So I'm hoping for the best.'

'The wine is magnificent, Matt. Everyone's going to love it. You can tell me all about it tomorrow.'

'This is an important night for me, Lauren. I want you with me.'

'Don't do this, please. I'd love to be there—you know that—and I'm flattered that you want me with you, but I can't let my mother find out we've been dating by suddenly showing up at the Club with you.'

'So tell her.'

'I will. But I need time.'

Matt's arms dropped to his sides and he shoved his hands into his pockets. 'You have as many excuses for not telling her about us as . . . as there are corks in these damned bottles. Don't you think this has gone far enough?'

'Don't be angry at me,' she pleaded.

He looked at her and sighed. 'I'm not angry at you,' he said finally. 'I'm angry at your mother.'

Lauren smiled slightly. 'Now you sound like her,' she teased. 'You barely know my mother. How can you be angry at her?'

'Because she's always crowded into the room with us, that's how.' He tucked a curl behind her ear. 'Did it ever occur to you that you might be handling this all wrong, sweetheart? You keep assuming that she's entitled to tell you how to live.'

'No, I don't.'

'Okay, maybe I'm overstating it. But you've come at this from the start as if she's the injured party. Think about it before you argue with me, Lauren,' he said, putting his finger lightly across her lips before she could speak. 'You took it for granted that you had to put her feelings before yours. And when she told you my father had done some awful thing to her years ago, you accepted it as truth.'

'I'm sure they saw it differently; I told you that, didn't I?'

'All I'm saying is that there are two sides to every story, Lauren,' he said, putting his hands on her shoulders. 'Your mother isn't always the good guy just because she's your mother.'

'Matt, for heaven's sake, I know that!'

'Then give my old man half a chance. Look, he's not the easiest person to deal with, but he's not a monster, either. And when he wants to, he can charm the birds out of the trees.' He smiled and ran his index finger down her nose. 'He asked about you on the phone last night.'

Lauren looked at him in disbelief. 'What?'

'He heard some kind of rumour. Don't look so frightened, love. It had to happen sooner or later.'

'And what did you tell him?' she asked quickly.

Matt grinned. 'I told him you don't know how to use chopsticks worth a damn . . .'

'Please don't tease me, Matt.'

'I told him you were wonderful—but that your mother hated his guts.'

'You didn't.'

'Don't look so upset. No, I was more subtle than that, but I did ask him if he remembered having a run-in with her, years ago.' Matt cupped her face in his hands. 'He didn't even know what I was talking about.'

Lauren sighed. He was simply confirming what she'd suspected all along.

'Look,' she said uncomfortably, 'I never said it was anything monumental.'

'I don't want to railroad you into this, but I think you'd better face facts, love. If my father's heard rumours about us, it's only a matter of time until your mother hears something, too. You know damned well it'll be better if she hears it from you.'

'Yes, but . . .'

'So it makes sense to tell her about me right now.

This afternoon, for instance,' he added with a quick grin. 'Then you can go with me tonight. I'll introduce you to my father—who knows? Maybe we can all end up having a drink together. How does that sound?'

'It sounds as if you've lost your mind,' Lauren said slowly. 'If you want something really exciting to happen tonight, why not see if you can arrange something simple, like an earthquake or a flood?' He laughed softly and drew her against him. 'You think I'm a coward, don't you?'

'Come with me, Lauren,' Matt urged softly. 'This is going to be an important night. I want you to share it with me.'

How could she deny him? she thought unhappily. He wanted her by his side, and she was behaving as if he had asked her to do something illicit. Moreover, what he had told her about his father having heard something about them was disturbing. It was going to be unpleasant enough telling her mother that she'd defied her all this time; if the information came to her from some gossipy acquaintance, it would be impossible. In her heart, Lauren knew it was time— past time, really—to get the whole thing into the open. She wanted to believe it was as simple as Matt made it sound, but a feeling of apprehension nagged at her.

'I'll tell her,' she said at last. 'And I'll go to the dance with you.' Matt's face softened with pleasure, and for an instant, her anxiety was soothed. But reality returned, and she sighed. 'I just wish . . . I just wish I could wave a magic wand and guarantee all this a happy ending.'

'We don't need any magic but the kind we feel when we're together.' His hands slipped from cupping her face to the back of her head, and he knotted his fingers in her long, thick hair. 'Trust me,' he murmured, leaning towards her.

'I do, Matt, but——'

His lips brushed over hers. 'But what?' he whispered huskily.

'But it all seems too simple . . .'

She sighed as his mouth touched her cheek as lightly as the wings of a butterfly stealing nectar from a flower.

'It is simple,' he assured her. 'I believe in simple things.'

Even now, driving the last few blocks toward the old frame house where her mother waited, Lauren could remember the heat of his hands as they slid under her shirt and spread across her naked back.

'I can't think when you do that,' she'd protested feebly. 'Matt . . . suppose someone comes in . . .'

'It's Saturday,' he'd whispered. 'There's no one here but you and me.'

A dazzling shaft of golden sunlight penetrated the darkness of the deserted shed, illuminating his face. She could see his love and need for her in the dark fire of his eyes, and when his mouth took hers and his hands found her breasts, she had tumbled willingly into the warm, dark void into which he led her.

CHAPTER NINE

AN hour later, freshly showered and wrapped in her towelling robe, Lauren sat facing her mother across the kitchen table. Evelyn Webster's hair was up in rollers, and her face was shiny with moisturiser.

'Primping for the dance,' she had said by way of explanation when Lauren came in. 'I took out your blue dress and pressed it,' she had added, her tone of voice almost defiant. 'I know you said you weren't going with me, but I hoped you might change your mind. It's still not too late, you know.'

Lauren's footsteps had faltered, and she had paused half way up the stairs to her room.

'As a matter of fact,' she'd said slowly, 'I—er—I did change my mind, Mother. I am going, after all.'

Her mother's delight made the truth even more difficult to tell, and Lauren found herself putting off what had to be done one last time. But there was no way to delay it any longer, she knew, as she sipped at a glass of fruit juice. It was best to get the thing over with. All she had to do was keep thinking of Matt and how much she loved him.

'You aren't eating, child. You really should, you know. They won't serve dinner until late this evening. That aspic's always been your favourite.'

Lauren managed a wavering smile and glanced down at her plate. A quivering mound of pale green jelly lay on it, glistening under the fluorescent light. She'd attempted one forkful, and the cold, slippery aspic had seemed to grow in her mouth until she was

certain she was going to be ill. Only determined
effort had finally got it down. Just the thought of
trying to swallow more of the stuff made her throat
constrict with nausea.

'I don't feel hungry, Mother,' she said, carefully
pushing her plate aside.

Her mother rose from the table. 'There's some rice
pudding . . .'

Lauren shuddered at the images conjured up by
the words. 'I think I had too much sun today,' she
said. 'The thought of food makes my stomach turn.'

Her mother glanced over her shoulder as she
stacked their dishes in the sink.

'I hope you didn't catch some kind of bug,
tramping around in the fields. It's ridiculous for a
secretary to be doing that kind of work.' She wiped
her hands on a small towel and then set two mugs on
the sink. 'I'm going to speak to Sunny Lane on
Monday, child. It seems to me you've been on loan to
that man's office long enough.'

Well, Lauren thought, there was no time like the
present. She took a deep breath and cleared her
throat.

'Mother, about Matthew Chandler . . .'

'Can you get the sugar canister, please, Lauren? I
can't reach it.'

'There's enough sugar in the bowl for now, isn't
there? Sit down, Mother. I . . . I want to talk to you.'

'In a minute, child. Let me just make some coffee
first.'

Nervousness put a sharp edge to Lauren's voice.
'The coffee can wait!'

Her mother looked at her in surprise. 'Whatever's
got into you, Lauren? Getting five seconds' worth of
conversation out of you these past few weeks has

been almost impossible, and now you're as impatient
as——'

'Please—sit down, Mother. I've got to tell you
something.'

The older woman hesitated and then pulled a chair
out from the table. 'Well, doesn't that sound serious!'
she said with a nervous laugh. 'What on earth is it,
child?'

Lauren folded her hands in her lap. They were cool
and damp. Easy, she warned herself. You aren't a
disobedient adolescent. You're a grown woman, and
you've done nothing to be ashamed of.

'It's . . . it's about Matthew Chandler and me,' she
said evenly. 'There isn't any easy way to tell you this.
I wish there were, but . . .' She took a deep breath.
'We . . . Matt and I . . . we've been seeing each
other.'

It was the kind of moment in which everything
seems to slow and become artificially bright. Lauren
was suddenly aware of the sharp sound of the clock
ticking on the wall and the faint, steady drip of water
into the sink.

'How long has this been going on?' Evelyn
Webster rasped.

'I know I should have told you sooner,' said
Lauren, fumbling for the right words. 'I wanted
to . . .'

Her mother's flat, cold stare seemed to pierce her
flesh. 'How long?' she repeated, waving aside
Lauren's stammered explanations.

Lauren swallowed past the lump that had formed
in her throat. Why did she suddenly feel as if she
were ten years old and caught with her hand in the
cookie jar? The fact that she'd been living a lie all
these weeks was as much her mother's fault as hers.

Evelyn had refused to hear the truth. She always refused to hear the truth. The only difference was that, in the past, her mother had had her own way.

'Most of the summer,' she said at last.

'Most of the . . .?'

Lauren nodded her head. 'I'm sorry I didn't tell you, right from the beginning. I tried, but—well, I . . . I guess I took the easy way out. It was a mistake, I know, but . . .'

'You lied and cheated and sneaked in and out of this house all that time?'

'Mother, listen to me!'

'Would you like to hear something really funny? Only yesterday, someone made a snide comment to me about you and . . . and that man, and I laughed.' Evelyn's mouth trembled and she shook her head. 'I said, don't be ridiculous, my daughter would never be foolish enough to be interested in someone like that. I said, she's just working for him, she has to, she has no choice.'

'If you'll just give me a chance to explain . . .'

'And, of course, I thought to myself, Lauren promised me she wouldn't ever see him again. She said she'd respect my wishes, she swore——'

'I didn't, Mother,' Lauren said quickly, trying to walk the fine line between assertion and conciliation. 'I said I wouldn't hurt you.'

Anger flashed in the older woman's eyes. 'Don't lie to me! You certainly did promise, that day we went shopping. You told me you wouldn't see that man again.'

'That isn't true. You heard what you wanted to hear that day, the way you always do when we disagree. I didn't promise anything of the sort.'

'Are you calling me a liar?'

Evelyn's voice rose in pitch and Lauren shook her head.

'No, no, of course not. It was a misunderstanding.'

Evelyn smiled bitterly. 'It certainly was. I assumed you'd show me some respect. I guess that shows how stupid I was.'

Lauren reached across the table and touched her mother's hand. 'Come on, Mother, you know I respect you. But that has nothing to do with what I feel for Matt.'

'And what precisely do you feel for *Matt*?' her mother asked hoarsely, spitting out the name with distaste.

Lauren hesitated. She wanted to keep to the truth and tell her mother that she loved him, but she knew instinctively that the moment was wrong. Her mother was as furious over what she saw as Lauren's duplicity as she was over Matt's intrusion into their lives. It was hardly the time to talk of love . . . No, this was the time to ease into things and give her mother a chance to accept what had happened.

'He's very important to me,' she said evenly.

"He's very important to me,' her mother mocked, her cheeks reddening under the translucent layer of cream. 'What kind of answer is that?' Her head shot forward like a snake's when it prepares to strike. 'You've been sleeping with that son of a bitch, haven't you?'

An angry blaze of crimson suffused Lauren's cheeks. 'How can you talk to me this way?'

'How? I'll tell you how!' Evelyn shouted. 'Because you lied to me all this time! You're capable of anything!'

'You made me lie to you,' Lauren bristled. 'You made me feel as if I always owed you explanations——'

Her mother's hand lashed out, and Lauren gasped in shock more than pain. Tears filled her eyes and she raised her fingers to her reddened cheek.

'Who do you think you're talking to?' Evelyn Webster demanded. 'You're damned right you owe me an explanation! What you do reflects on me . . . I'll just bet this whole town is laughing behind my back. No wonder Sunny Lane looked as if I had two heads when I asked her how much longer you'd have to work in that man's office. What a fool she must have thought I was!'

Lauren shook her head in disbelief. There it was, even now, even when she was trying to make her mother understand something so important.

'That's all you ever think of, isn't it?' she spluttered, wiping away her tears with the back of her hand. 'You, and your precious standing in San Jacinto. What about me and my feelings?'

'How dare you ask me that? Haven't I spent my entire life worrying about you? I thought you understood, that day we went shopping together. But I might as well have been talking to myself. You didn't listen to one thing, did you? You simply sat there, yessing me to death, knowing all the while you were going to do exactly what you pleased, when you pleased . . .'

'That isn't true,' Lauren said angrily. 'I listened to every word, but you refused to hear what I was saying. I wanted to tell you—I tried to tell you—but you were so damned busy thinking about yourself and your precious ego! How could you expect me to hate Matt because of some stupid fight you had with his father years ago?'

'I was trying to make you understand what kind of

people the Chandlers are, Lauren.'

'Oh, for heaven's sake, Mother, I know what kind of people they are.'

Her mother smiled unpleasantly. 'Is that a fact?'

'I know what kind Matt is, anyway. He's good and kind and decent . . .'

'How touching,' her mother said, her voice weighted with sarcasm.

'You may not like hearing it, but it's the truth. If you'd only give him half a chance . . .'

Evelyn Webster pushed back from the table and got heavily to her feet. 'No one in this town likes that old man,' she said, walking to the sink and filling the kettle. 'Oh, lots of people pretend they do, but they don't. Even Millie Harrow . . .'

Lauren slapped her hand on the table. 'Do you know how crazy this sounds? Since when does my life have to depend on who Millie Harrow likes or dislikes?' She snatched up her plate and emptied it into the garbage. 'Anyway, we aren't talking about Arthur Chandler, we're talking about Matt.'

'Let's talk about him, then. I find it amazing that Matthew Chandler is the only man in town who interests you, Lauren. There are certainly others.'

Lauren took a deep breath. 'No, there aren't,' she said at last, her words low and controlled. 'I've never felt this way about anyone else, Mother.'

'You haven't given yourself a chance,' her mother said impatiently.

'That's why I disobeyed you. You know I never have before.'

'That doesn't excuse it,' her mother said sharply.

'I'm not trying to excuse it,' Lauren said quietly. 'I just want you to understand.'

Evelyn Webster snorted. 'I understand,' she said sharply, mindlessly spooning instant coffee into two mugs. 'You disobeyed me.'

'Mother . . .'

'You ruined your reputation.'

'Mother, for God's sake, this is the twentieth century . . .'

'And for what? For a . . . a squalid little affair!'

'Stop it!' snapped Lauren, her cheeks colouring. 'You can't make this into something dirty. I won't let you.'

'Why this sudden devotion to truth? You've done whatever you wanted all along; why are you telling me now? I gather you have no intention of breaking this . . . this relationship off?'

Lauren nodded. 'That's right, Mother.'

Evelyn folded her arms in front of her. 'Were you afraid that I'd hear about it from someone else?'

'That's part of it,' she admitted, sighing as she settled into a chair, 'although Matt begged me to tell you about us a long time ago.'

'Did he, now?' the older woman asked suspiciously.

'Yes, he——'

'Well, you've told me,' Evelyn interrupted abruptly, setting two mugs of coffee on the table. 'Now what?'

Lauren caught her lower lip between her teeth. 'I want to . . .' She cleared her throat and began again. 'I intend to date Matt openly from now on, Mother. He wants to be able to come to the house to call for me . . .'

Evelyn's lip curled. 'How touching!'

Don't pick up the challenge, Lauren told herself.

Don't get caught up in a petty squabble over words and implications.

'It may not sound like much, but we've never so much as gone to a restaurant together in San Jacinto. We've been so careful . . . at least, we thought we had. But today, Matt told me his father asked about me——'

The sound of her mother's indrawn breath was a loud rasp in the quiet room. 'His father asked about you?' she repeated slowly.

Lauren nodded. 'He heard a rumour, I guess.' She ran her fingertip slowly around the lip of her mug. 'You know, Matt said he didn't even remember quarrelling with you years ago.'

The older woman's laugh was brittle.

'There was a time I'd have been very upset to hear that,' she said. 'But I'm not the fool I once was. I'm not surprised; I'm sure he forgot all about me in no time at all.' She lifted her mug to her lips and sipped the rapidly cooling coffee. 'So he didn't remember, hmm? Then I guess he didn't tell his son to stop seeing you.'

'You mean the way you told me not to see Matt?' Lauren asked. 'No, he didn't.' For a second, she almost smiled. The thought of Arthur Chandler telling Matt who he could and couldn't date was preposterous enough; did her mother really think anybody but she would carry an old grudge to such extremes?

Evelyn set her mug down. 'You still haven't told me why you decided to make a clean breast of things today, Lauren.' Her lips narrowed with distaste. 'It certainly isn't because you wanted my permission to see Matthew Chandler. You've made it clear that you're going to flaunt your relationship whether I like it or not. If it was to try and clear your guilty conscience, I can't help you. I disapprove, and nothing will change my mind about that. If you insist on having him come to the house to call for you, don't expect me to . . .'

Here we go, Lauren thought. The best was yet to come.

'The reason I told you today is because . . . because Matt's asked me to go to the dance with him tonight.' Her mother looked at her blankly. 'It's an important night for him, and he wants me there. And there was no way we could work that out unless I told you everything . . .'

Her mother's eyes searched her face. 'Let me get this straight,' she said slowly. 'Matthew Chandler wants to take you to the dance tonight?'

Lauren nodded. 'He . . . he wants me to meet his father, too. He's going to be there.'

Evelyn pushed against the table and got to her feet. 'Do what you want, Lauren. I don't want to hear it—I don't want any part of it.'

Lauren rose and followed her into the hall. 'Don't walk out on me, Mother. You're going to have to deal with this, sooner or later.'

'I will not,' the older woman said coldly, starting up the steps towards her bedroom. 'If you want to make a fool of yourself . . .'

'I want to be Matt's wife!'

The words, torn from the deepest recesses of Lauren's heart, hung in the air, as much a surprise to her as they were to her mother. Evelyn Webster turned, her hand to her throat.

'I love him,' Lauren whispered, 'and he loves me.'

Her mother stared at her. 'He's told you that?' Lauren nodded. 'And he's proposed to you?'

'Not yet—not in so many words—but I know he will. Why else would he want me to be with him tonight? That's why I want you to accept him, Mother. Please, please give him a chance.'

A mix of emotions flashed across Evelyn's face. 'Lauren . . .' She closed her eyes and shook her head. 'Lauren, there are so many things you don't understand . . .'

'You're right,' said Lauren, her voice breaking. 'I don't understand anything. Why don't you want me to be happy?' She brushed her hand across her eyes and glared at her mother. 'You don't have any answers, do you?'

'Lauren, child——' Evelyn began, holding out her arms imploringly.

'I am not a child!' Lauren snapped angrily. 'That's the problem, isn't it? You want me to have a child's loyalty, a child's blind obedience. Somebody stepped on your toes years ago, so I'm expected to make that person my enemy, too.'

'No, no . . . Lauren . . .'

'I'm supposed to be a good little girl who makes sure her mother approves of all her friends. Well, I'm not a little girl any more. I'm a woman, and I love Matthew Chandler.' She hesitated as she looked at her mother's pale face. 'That doesn't mean I don't love you, Mother,' she said softly. 'I don't want to hurt you, but . . .'

The implied threat hung between them, as fragile as a single gossamer strand spun by a spider. Finally, Evelyn sighed.

'All right, Lauren,' she murmured. 'We'll try it your way. I don't want to hurt you, either.' She reached out and smoothed Lauren's hair back from her flushed cheeks, then she smiled faintly. 'Oh, the things we do for love,' she said in a bitter whisper.

Only later would Lauren realise the true meaning of those words.

CHAPTER TEN

LAUREN glanced at her mother as she pulled her car into a parking space at the Country Club. They had made the drive in silence; in fact, although they'd hugged tearfully after their argument, they'd spent the balance of the afternoon in a guarded silence, comprised of one part Lauren's anxiety about the evening ahead and one part Evelyn Webster's realisation that she could no longer exercise the same control over her daughter. Each of them sensed the other's feelings; it was the reason Lauren had chosen not to force a face-to-face meeting between her mother and Matt until the last possible minute. She felt she owed the older woman at least that much.

Late in the afternoon, she had telephoned him. Even such a simple act had thrilled her: it was the first time she had ever called him from her own home.

'I told her,' she'd whispered softly.

'Terrific,' he'd said happily. 'What colour is her dress? I'll bring flowers for the both of you ...'

'Meet us at the Club,' she'd pleaded. 'It'll be easier for her.'

He'd grumbled about it, but finally he had agreed. Now, as Lauren and her mother walked into the ballroom, she was doubly glad she had insisted on these arrangements. She was so nervous that her stomach felt as if it were floating; if Matt had been with her, she doubted if she'd have been able to walk. She took her mother's arm, and Evelyn gave her a quick, artificial smile. I know just how she feels, Lauren thought. Everything was happening too quickly. After months of avoiding anybody who might recognise them, she and Matt were about to bring all the principal players together . . .

She felt her mother's arm tremble in hers. 'You did a marvellous job with the decorations,' Lauren said quickly, hoping to calm her.

Evelyn nodded stiffly. 'I was only part of the committee . . .' Her words drifted off into silence. 'Look, there's Millie Harrow,' she said suddenly. It was impossible not to hear the relief in her voice. 'I'm sitting at her table. We were both supposed to, you know. You remember, I told you about her nephew?' She sighed and shook her head. 'I'm babbling, aren't I? Lauren, I hope to God you know what you're doing . . .'

Lauren squeezed her mother's hand. 'Don't worry, please.'

'I just don't want you to get hurt.'

'We've been all through this, Mother.'

'Lauren . . .'

'I want to find Matt,' Lauren said deliberately. 'I'll make my apologies to Mrs Harrow later.'

How calm and steady she sounded, Lauren thought in amazement. She'd said that as if being seen in public with Matthew Chandler was the most normal thing in the world, instead of the monumental event she knew it was. After tonight, everyone would know about them . . . A tremor of excitement rippled through her; at the same second, the one mouthful of aspic she'd managed to eat at lunch seemed to leap into her throat. She swayed as the blood rushed from her head.

'What's the matter?' her mother asked sharply.

'Are you all right?'

Lauren nodded, not trusting herself to speak.

'You're as white as a ghost. I told you to eat something, Lauren. You're always dieting.'

'I'm okay now,' she murmured. 'It's just a little warm in here. Oh, there's Matt!'

Seeing him made her feel better. How handsome he looked in his dinner jacket! He was scanning the room—looking for her, she realised happily—and she smiled as she caught his eye and waved. His face lit up as he saw her and started towards them.

'My God, child, you're going to crush my fingers,' her mother whispered, tugging her hand free of Lauren's. 'Take it easy.'

Lauren murmured an apology. It was good advice; she felt like an overstretched rubber band. The slightest pull and she'd snap. But how could she feel otherwise on a night such as this?

'Hello,' Matt said softly. 'You look beautiful.'

She blushed and gave him a smile that excluded everyone else. 'Thank you,' she murmured. Beside her, Evelyn stirred and cleared her throat. 'Umm, Mother, I'd like you to meet Matthew Chandler.' The statement struck her as ludicrous, and she fought back an almost overwhelming desire to laugh. Nerves, she thought desperately, just nerves . . . Control yourself, Lauren. She took a deep breath and began again. 'I guess you two know each other, come to think of it, but . . .' Her stumbling introduction drifted into silence. 'This is the toughest thing I've ever had to do,' she said bluntly, 'and I'm doing it badly.'

Matt slipped his arm around her waist. 'You're doing fine,' he murmured, and then he smiled at her mother. 'It's a pleasure to see you, Mrs Webster,' he said, holding his hand out to her. 'I'm sorry our meeting has been delayed.' Lauren held her breath. There was a detached expression on her mother's face as she stared at Matt. Finally she placed her hand in his and withdrew it almost immediately.

'Mr Chandler,' she said politely. 'It was nice of you to invite my daughter to the Club tonight.'

Matt smiled and his arm tightened around Lauren. 'I wouldn't have dreamed of coming without her, Mrs Webster.'

Her mother smiled coolly. 'Yes, so she said. Well, she's old enough to make her own decisions.'

Lauren looked from Matt to her mother. Both of them wore polite, neutral expressions on their faces, and their voices were pleasantly pitched, but her mother's hostility was almost palpable.

'Why don't you tell my mother about your Chardonnay?' she asked nervously.

Matt gave her a quick, grateful smile. 'Yes, you might be interested, Mrs Webster. We imported the rootstock from France . . .'

'Really?' her mother said coldly. 'You must tell me about it some time. Lauren, I'm going to Millie's table now. Please don't forget your manners; she'll be expecting you to stop by and say hello.' She nodded coolly at Matt. 'Good evening, Mr Chandler.'

Matt's arm tightened warningly around Lauren's waist. She kept quiet until her mother had wound her way across the dance floor to the Harrow table, and then she shook her head.

'I'm sorry, Matt,' she said unhappily. 'I hoped she'd be nice.'

'She was polite, wasn't she? At least, she talked to me.' He smiled down at her. 'Come on, lady. You can't expect miracles the first time out.'

'No, I suppose not,' Lauren admitted. 'I guess it wasn't so bad.' She glanced around the room and leaned closer to him. 'Is your father here yet?'

'No, not yet.' He chuckled softly. 'He'll be a pushover, compared to your mother.'

'I hope you're right,' she said slowly.

'I am,' Matt said positively. 'He's the type who tells you exactly what he's thinking—and he can think only good things about us.'

Doubt and hope were mirrored in Lauren's eyes. 'I hope you're right . . .'

'Of course I'm right,' he said positively. 'You're as pale as a ghost, love. Are you feeling all right?'

'Of course,' she lied, although a sudden wave of nausea had clutched at her again. 'I'm just nervous.'

'I know a way to relax you,' Matt said softly. He chuckled as a blush spread across her face. 'A public way, you wanton. Remember the first night we met? We danced on the terrace then. How would you like to try the dance floor this time?'

She glanced over his shoulder at the still empty dance floor. 'Don't you think we should wait until someone else is out there?'

His answer was to lead her to the centre of the polished hardwood floor and draw her into his arms.

'Everyone is watching,' she whispered, trying unsuccessfully to maintain some distance between them.

'Let them watch,' he whispered, his breath warm against her ear.

'Yes, but what will they think?'

'Do you really care?' he asked softly.

His hand moved up her back and into her hair. With a sigh, she laid her head on his shoulder and tried to let the tension flow from her body. He was right, she thought. There was no reason to feel uncomfortable. All that mattered was Matt . . . Still, she felt a quick, feathery flutter of guilt when she glimpsed her mother's pale face as she whirled by the Harrow table in Matt's arms. She knew other faces were watching, with eyes fixed and intense. San Jacinto would be buzzing tomorrow.

Other couples finally joined them, but she began to relax only when the music changed from slow and romantic to wild and frenetic, and she and Matt drew apart as they danced.

'You've got some interesting moves there, Mr Chandler,' she said breathlessly. 'I was afraid you might not be able to keep up with me.'

'Oh, you'll pay for that remark, woman. You haven't seen anything yet . . . Lauren? What is it?'

She reached out blindly and grabbed his outstretched hand. Everything was suddenly out of focus . . .

'I . . . I don't know,' she stammered, trying to gulp air into her lungs. 'I just got dizzy for a minute. I'm fine now . . .'

'Are you sure? Do you want me to carry you?'

'God, no,' she whispered. 'Imagine what a sensation that would make! If we could just sit down for a while . . .'

Matt put his arm around her waist and led her slowly to the Chandler table.

'Do you want to step outside for a breath of fresh air?'

She shook her head, although the motion made her stomach roll. 'No, I'm fine,' she lied, certain that she'd never be able to walk far enough to reach the terrace. 'I just want to sit down. That's it,' she said with relief, as she sank into a chair. 'Don't look so worried.'

Matt slipped into the chair next to hers and took her hands in his. 'I am worried, Lauren. What happened just now?'

She smiled weakly. 'Nothing terribly dramatic. I think I'm just hungry. That's what my mother says, anyway, and she's probably right. Mothers are, sometimes.'

'When did you eat last?'

'I . . . I don't remember,' she said shamefacedly. 'I know I had some tea this morning, and some crackers and cheese around noon . . .'

Matt frowned and reached for the basket of bread and rolls in the centre of the table.

'That's not enough eating, for God's sake. Have one of these rolls while I scout up something more substantial. They must have some *hors d'oeuvre* left from the cocktail hour.'

Lauren tugged at his sleeve as he half rose from his seat. 'You wouldn't be that cruel,' she whispered. 'You wouldn't really force me to eat those awful things, would you? I missed the cocktail hour fair and square . . .' He hesitated and she forced a smile to her lips. 'I'll eat the roll. I promise. Anyway, they'll serve dinner soon.'

'I don't know, sweetheart,' he said slowly. 'Maybe I should get Dr Howell over here. I saw him earlier.'

'Matt, please! I feel conspicuous enough as it is. I swear to you, I'm fine—really.'

He stared at her doubtfully and then sighed. 'All right, Lauren. But you'd better eat every morsel they serve tonight.'

The very thought of eating made her throat constrict. 'I thought you loved me,' she said lightly.

'How can you condemn me to such a fate?'

'That's true,' he grinned, taking both her hands in his and holding them tightly. 'Well, then, promise to eat a little. We can drive into San Francisco later for crab at the Wharf or ice cream in Ghiradelli Square . . .'

'I don't think so,' she whispered, suppressing a shudder. 'I think I'm coming down with something. Don't look so upset, for heaven's sake. It's just one of those twenty-four hour bugs I always seem to get in the fall.'

'Then I definitely should get Dr Howell over here.'

Her glance skittered past Matt and her eyes widened. 'Oh, God . . . Matt, your father is here! He just came in. Are you sure he'll like me? I hope my mother doesn't do anything foolish. I . . .'

She swallowed her nervous outburst and took a deep breath as Matt rose to his feet to greet his father. Lauren had seen Arthur Chandler before, of course. Even though he'd announced his retirement from the day to day business of running the winery some months earlier, he still came to work several days a week. He was Matt's height, and had the same broad-shouldered, narrow-waisted build. Looking at him was like looking at Matt forty years hence, she thought. Only their eyes were different: Matt's were a dark, almost smoky blue, while the elder Chandler's were pale and icy. Forcing a smile to her face, she scrambled to her feet as Matt introduced them.

'How do you do, Mr Chandler. I've heard so much about you.'

'From your mother?' he asked with a smile.

'No, not really,' she said quickly. What a stupid remark to have made, she thought. Well, he'd smiled, at least . . . Not that it had reached his eyes, she noticed. 'I . . . Matt thought I should come tonight, Mr Chandler. I hope you don't mind.'

'Of course not, Miss Webster. When Matt told me he was going to ask you here this evening, I knew it was important to make your acquaintance.'

There was that same smile again. It was proper, charming—but it stopped far short of the man's eyes. She glanced at Matt, wondering if he'd noticed. Noticed what? She asked herself. No one, not even Matt, had ever claimed Arthur Chandler had a warm personality. Charming when he wanted to be, Matt had said, and indeed, he was being charming, engaging in conversation first with her and then with Matt. He'd just said something to her, she realised, although her nervousness had made her mind wander.

'. . . fine chance for us to chat. You don't mind, do you, Miss Webster?'

'Call me Lauren, please,' she said quickly. 'I'm sorry; I seem to have missed what you were saying.'

'That's all right, my dear. It was all viticulture anyway, although Matthew tells me you're quite knowledgeable.'

Was it her imagination, or was there an unctuous edge to the man's voice, a curious shading to the innocent words? Again, she glanced at Matt; one look at his face and she knew he was worried about something.

'Matt? What is it?' she said anxiously.

'Darling, you're going to have to forgive me. My father said the sommelier stopped him as he was coming in and told him there's some problem with my Chardonnay. They've either delivered the wrong bottles or they've misplaced them.'

'How could that happen, Matt? Didn't you

supervise the loading yourself?'

He shrugged. 'I don't know, Lauren. I'll have to go sort it out.'

For some unaccountable reason, a chill seemed to dance down her spine.

'I'll go with you,' she said quickly.

'And leave me here all alone, Miss Webster? You wouldn't do that to an old man, would you?' Chandler asked lightly. 'Besides, I suspect that Matthew will have to take a run back to the winery. Surely you don't want me to dine all by myself?'

Matt looked uncertainly from Lauren to his father. 'Lauren, I . . .'

'You go on,' she said quickly, although she wanted to clutch at his arm for safety. 'Take care of the wine.' His eyes met hers and she nodded. 'I'll be fine, really.'

'Of course she will, Matthew. I'll take proper care of her, I promise.'

Matt bent and brushed his lips against hers. She smiled and squeezed his hand, then watched as he hurried through the room and out of the door. Her mother was staring at her from across the dance floor. She could almost hear her mother's thoughts—as far as she was concerned, her daughter was giving aid and comfort to the enemy.

'It looks as if we're going to have this entire table all to ourselves,' she said with forced brightness. 'Either that, or everyone else is very late.'

'I arranged our seating, Miss Webster, just as soon as I confirmed the rumours I heard about you and my son.'

Lauren flushed. 'That we'd been seeing each other? Yes, Matt told me. I'm sorry you had to hear it that way. Won't you please call me Lauren?'

Arthur Chandler smiled. 'I'd much rather keep our relationship as impersonal as possible, Miss Webster. Our business will be simpler to conduct that way.'

His voice had become cold and brittle. Lauren stared at him in silence while the waiter served their first course, and then she cleared her throat nervously.

'Have I . . . have I done something to offend you, Mr Chandler?'

'Miss Webster, we have no time to waste on preliminaries. I had no intention whatsoever of handling this—unpleasantness—this evening, but your presence here leaves me no choice.'

What on earth was he talking about? She put down her spoon and leaned towards him.

'Look, I don't know what you mean,' she said in low, urgent tones. 'Matt wanted us to meet——'

'I understand you told Matthew you know nothing of what happened to your mother years ago,' Chandler smiled. 'I'm half tempted to believe you, Miss Webster. You have such a convincingly innocent look on your face, you see, but what's the difference, after all? Whether your mother's part of this or not, you aren't going to succeed. You are going to stop seeing my son.'

I'm having a bad dream, Lauren thought. The idea was so convincing that she almost sighed with relief. Of course, that was it. This was a nightmare, a frighteningly real one. She'd had them before—everyone had—and once you knew it was nothing but a dream, all you had to do was concentrate on that fact and you'd wake up safe in your own bed.

But this was no dream. The sounds and smells of the ballroom were the stuff of reality, not of the mind. Lauren pushed her chair back so suddenly that it squealed in protest. She had to find Matt.

'You won't be able to find my son, Miss Webster,' Chandler said, as if her thoughts were transparent. 'I've seen to it that the problem with his Chardonnay is a fairly complicated one. I'm afraid he's going to find that he must return to the winery to solve it. We're going to have all the time we need for our chat.'

How polite and courteous he sounded—and how pleasant he looked, Lauren thought in amazement. Anyone watching them would think they were having a perfectly normal conversation.

'Are you as good an actress as I think, Miss Webster? Can you maintain your composure, or shall we go out on the terrace?'

She licked her suddenly dry lips and shook her head. It would be impossible to leave the room, she knew. She was sure she'd never make it to the door without fainting.

'What . . . what is this all about?' she whispered.

The old man drew his chair closer to the table. 'I want you to stay away from my son,' he said coldly. 'I know what comes next in this little scenario: you're assuming Matthew will ask you to marry him.'

'That's none of your business, Mr Chandler,' she said weakly.

'Don't be a fool!' the old man snapped. 'Of course it's my business. I don't know how you sustained my son's interest in you this long, or how you plan on springing your trap.'

Lauren pushed back from the table, the instinct for self-preservation making her want to flee.

'I don't have to listen to this . . .'

'. . . unless you intend to take a page from your

mother's book. Believe me, it won't work. I won't let it.'

She sagged back into her chair, her eyes fastened on Chandler's face like a bird mesmerised by a snake.

'What does my mother have to do with this?' she whispered.

The old man reached for a bottle of red wine that had been left open. 'Not a bad Zinfandel,' he said, passing the cork under his nose. 'Well, not as good as a Chandler. May I pour you some?'

'I asked you what my mother has to do with this, Mr Chandler.'

Chandler held the glass of dark red wine up to eye level. 'The vintner who produced this wine knows its lineage. He can document its rootstock for generations.' He placed the glass on the table and his eyes met hers. 'The wine has a history, Miss Webster. You only have a past.'

'People like you make me sick!' she snapped, anger suddenly infusing her with strength. 'Just because we're not one of San Jacinto's old, wealthy families, we're . . . Pedigrees are for viniculture, Mr Chandler, not for people.' She tossed her napkin on the table. 'I don't have to sit here and listen to this drivel. When Matt gets back——'

She was halfway out of her chair when Arthur Chandler's fingers closed around her wrist.

'Listen very carefully, Miss Webster,' he said quietly, his eyes cold stones that drew her. 'You're a bastard, born out of wedlock and denied by your father.'

Lauren slid back into her seat as the room spun up and away, the burgundy and pink blending into a kaleidoscope of colourful shards and pieces. There was a roaring noise in her head and a sharp taste in her mouth. Don't pass out, you fool, she raged inwardly. Count the silverware and the threads in the tablecloth ... do whatever you must, but don't get sick. Take a deep breath. That's the way. Now take another ...

'You're a liar!' she flung at him. 'My father died in Vietnam ...'

'He certainly did, but he was only there because he thought the Army was preferable to marrying your mother. This town's believed her story for years—the brave young widow raising her child alone—because I let it.' His voice lowered and turned harsh. 'Tell me, young woman, what do you think would happen to your mother's precious respectability if it knew the truth? We both know how important status is to her, and how precarious her acceptance has been.'

'I don't believe you,' said Lauren in a low voice.

The old man smiled. 'Ask your mother, my dear. Let her tell you about the handsome settlement I gave her on behalf of her young man. If you have any regard for her, you'll give my son up at once.'

'That's extortion,' Lauren said faintly. 'What do you think Matt will say when I tell him you're blackmailing me?'

'If you tell him,' Arthur Chandler said, giving heavy emphasis to the word. 'But why would you, Miss Webster? We both know he'd curse me and walk out. He'd leave the land and the business he's devoted his life to. And I'd certainly have nothing to lose at that point; I'd see to it everyone knew about your—how shall we put it?—your parentage. Just think of the repercussions, Miss Webster. Your mother would lose everything, Matthew would lose everything ...' He shrugged his shoulders. 'So would you, eventually. You might be enough for my son for a while, but sooner or later, he'd regret the loss of the land, the winery, the life he's led. How long do you think your relationship would survive then?'

Her mother had warned her about Arthur Chandler, but nothing had prepared her for the vicious cruelty of the man. His smiling face swam before her eyes. She knew she had to get up and get out of the room, even if it took her last ounce of strength. Chandler was still grasping her wrist; she pulled her hand free and almost staggered as she got to her feet. A cold beading of sweat rose on her forehead and a strange, prickling sensation spread into her hands and feet. She took a deep breath and started across the room. The exit door seemed far away ... there was an endless distance to navigate before she reached it. And the floor was shifting beneath her feet.

You're going to make it, she told herself. You must ... you can do it. Just put one foot down, and then the other, that's the way, one foot, then the other ... But the damned floor moved again, as if it were made of jelly, and suddenly she was falling, falling ...

Lauren's eyes fluttered open. She was lying on a couch in a small office. She groaned and tried to sit up, but the movement made her stomach lurch.

'Easy, young lady, easy. Don't move too quickly ...'

'Dr Howell? What happened?'

The physician helped her to a sitting position. 'You tell me, Lauren. You fainted out there. Your mother is frantic. I'm going to have to let her in here in a second, before she breaks down the door!'

Lauren smiled weakly. 'I guess I scared the heck out of her. It's okay, doctor. You can let her in.'

'Not just yet,' the doctor said, sitting down next to her. 'I'd like you to come in for a complete check-up, Lauren. I've only done the preliminaries here.'

'I'm fine, really. I haven't eaten since this afternoon, or maybe I'm coming down with something.'

The doctor shifted uncomfortably. 'Lauren, when was the last time you menstruated?'

The directness of the question hit her like a spray of cold water. 'I . . . God, I'm not sure . . . I . . .'

Her eyes widened with fear. Dr Howell nodded sympathetically and reached over and patted her hand.

'Come in tomorrow,' he said softly, 'and I'll do a complete work-up. But I don't think there's much doubt about it, Lauren. I'm afraid all signs suggest that you're pregnant.'

CHAPTER ELEVEN

Two hours later, their faces haggard with exhaustion, Lauren and her mother sat facing each other across the kitchen table. The romantic story of her parents' wartime elopement lay between them, a shattered myth.

'How could you have lied to me all these years?' Lauren asked, her voice a hoarse whisper in the quiet room.

'I wanted to protect you, child,' Evelyn Webster said wearily. 'I've explained and explained . . . I was barely eighteen years old and I made a mistake. There was no reason to involve you.'

'You must be joking, Mother! I've been involved in this all my life, even though I didn't know a damned thing about it. Besides, it was ridiculous to feed me all that nonsense about Arthur Chandler keeping you from a promotion.'

Her mother's head sprang up. 'Those were your words, Lauren. I simply said he'd changed the course of my life.'

'And what an understatement that was,' Lauren said bitterly. 'But he didn't do it by himself, Mother. He had plenty of help from my . . . from my father. What I still can't figure out is how you could have got involved with someone like that. I know how you feel about people who have money . . .'

'Watch what you say to me, Lauren!' Evelyn said sharply. 'I don't have to justify my behaviour to you.' She sighed and her tone softened. 'I thought I loved

152

your father, child. He seemed so exciting—I admit, maybe part of it was because he came from a wealthy Santa Clara family, but he was handsome and fun and——' She shrugged her shoulders and got to her feet. 'We've been all through this.'

'Tell me again,' Lauren said quietly.

'Why, for God's sake? What's the point?'

'You let me believe in a lie all my life. I'm sorry,' Lauren said quickly. 'I know how hard this must be for you, but it isn't any easier for me, Mother. I'm trying my best to understand. Tell me the story again, please.'

Evelyn sighed and leaned wearily against the sink. 'All right,' she said at last. 'But this is the last time, child. I . . . I went to a dance in Santa Clara with some friends one night, and I met him. He . . . I guess you'd say he swept me off my feet,' she sighed, filling the kettle with water. 'He said he loved me—otherwise, I wouldn't have . . . well, what does it matter? We saw each other for several months, and then I found out I was . . . I was pregnant.'

Lauren shuddered at the word. What was the saying about the sins of the fathers being visited upon their sons? Could you say the same thing about mothers and daughters?

'And you never met his family?'

'No, of course not. He never even wanted us to be around his friends. He said he just wanted us to be alone together, and I believed—Look, how many more times must we——'

'I'm not trying to open old wounds for you, Mother,' Lauren said quickly. 'It's just that . . . that . . . She shrugged helplessly. 'I guess I don't have any more questions.'

In truth, she had lots more, but there wasn't

anything to be gained by asking them. Her mother—
her proper, controlled mother—had made an incredible error in judgment and had paid for it all her
life. No wonder she hated Arthur Chandler . . . and
no wonder she feared the consequences of Lauren's
involvement with his son.

But mothers and daughters weren't always the
same, after all. Her life and her mother's would
branch in two completely different directions. Matt
wanted to marry her. She knew he did; everything he
had said and done pointed in that direction.

Both women jumped as the piercing shriek of the
kettle filled the kitchen.

'It isn't a very pretty story,' her mother said as she
spooned instant coffee into both cups and then filled
them with water from the kettle. 'But I thought your
father wanted to marry me—he never said so, not in
so many words, but I just assumed . . . and then,
when I told him I was pregnant, he said . . . he said
he thought I'd been smarter than that. He said I'd
have to get rid of it . . . Of you,' she added with
sudden ferocity, her eyes bright with remembered
anger. 'He said he knew a place . . .' The anger
drained out of her words and she sank into her chair.
'. . . I just couldn't do it . . . I had nowhere to turn,
child.'

'Couldn't you have told Grandfather?'

'No, no . . . I couldn't have burdened him. Your
grandmother had died only months before, and he
was lost without her.' Evelyn Webster rubbed at a
drop of spilled coffee. 'I begged Jim—your father—
to marry me but he just laughed at the idea. I was
desperate, Lauren; I told him I was going to his
parents to tell them everything.'

'And that's when Arthur Chandler came into the

picture?'

Her mother nodded. 'I'd just started work at the winery, and he sent for me. I thought it was about my job, but . . . the rich stick together, Lauren,' she said with a bitter smile. 'Make no mistake about that. It turned out he was Jim's godfather; your father must have panicked when I threatened to go to his folks, and he ran to Chandler for help.' She wrapped her hands around her coffee cup as if seeking its warmth. 'He told me Jim was gone and I'd never see him again.'

'You mean he'd joined the Army,' Lauren prompted.

Her mother set her cup down and nodded. 'Arthur Chandler handed me an envelope with more money in it than I'd ever seen. He said it was enough so I could move to San Francisco and have my baby. I . . . I said I'd do it, but that I wanted to come back. I couldn't raise my child alone, away from the only home I'd ever known, and he finally agreed to give me a job when I returned . . .' Her eyes met Lauren's. 'I didn't want to take his money, but what else could I do?' she said pleadingly. 'I had no choice . . .'

'I'm not judging you, Mother,' Lauren said softly, reaching across the table and squeezing her mother's hand. 'No one has that right.' Especially not me, she thought, especially not now. 'What did you tell Grandfather?'

'I told him I wanted to try living in the city. After a while, I called home and said I'd fallen madly in love with a soldier—William Webster, I called him—and I said there hadn't been time for anything but an elopement because he was shipping out to Vietnam. Then, just before your birth, I said he'd been killed, and it was true in a way. I found out later that Jim had died there.' Evelyn sighed wearily. 'I'm not sure your grandfather ever really believed me, but you know how good and kind he was, child. He took us in and loved us both.'

Lauren sighed and leaned back in the hard wooden chair. 'Well, at least the way you feel about Arthur Chandler makes sense now. I just wish I'd known.'

Her mother wiped her eyes. 'I never wanted you to find out. It was my burden, not yours.'

Lauren leaned heavily on the table and got to her feet. She felt as if she had aged decades in the past few hours.

'I was thinking of the conversation I had with Matt's father tonight, Mother. I . . . I'd have been prepared for it.'

'I never dreamed that son of a bitch would do something like this,' her mother said softly. 'When you told me that he knew about you and his son, I thought . . . I mean, Arthur Chandler never went in for subtlety. If he hadn't said anything to Matthew, I figured it meant he'd forgotten or that the years had mellowed him.' She paused and then lifted her chin and squared her shoulders. 'I know you think I've been a grovelling fool all these years, Lauren . . .'

'Mother . . .'

Evelyn held up her hand. 'It's okay. Really it is. I did what I thought I had to do for you, child.' Her eyes glistened fiercely. 'And I did it, didn't I? Isn't it incredible, when you think about it? That son of a bitch is so afraid of my daughter that he's had to threaten us!'

Lauren sighed. 'You know me, Mother. I don't really give a damn what anybody thinks. Anyway, it's pretty outdated gossip. All we'd have to do is look everybody in the eye.' She looked at her mother and squeezed her hand lightly. 'It would probably be harder for you than it would for me.'

Evelyn snorted. 'I told you, it doesn't matter. I wanted you to have a better life than I had.' She blushed and a sly look flashed across her face. 'And you'll have that, if you marry Matthew Chandler. I know you think that's a terrible thing to say,' she added quickly, 'but it's true.'

'Mother!'

'I know he hasn't asked you yet, but it's only a matter of time. I watched him tonight. Lauren, you know I wanted to believe the worst about him, but even I have to admit I was wrong.'

Lauren took a deep breath and then exhaled slowly. 'I wish I didn't have to tell him. Oh, not that I'm ... you know, about my birth, but about what happened between me and his father. I'm afraid things will happen just the way Arthur Chandler predicted, and Matt will walk out on everything he loves.'

Her words drifted and dissipated like smoke in still air. Had sanity left her? Here she sat, agonising over the consequences of the old man's revelations for everybody but herself and the child she was certainly carrying. And there was no doubt in her mind that she was, indeed, pregnant. There had been changes in her body these past weeks, changes she'd somehow chosen to ignore.

Evelyn Webster cleared her throat and shifted her spare frame in the hard kitchen chair.

'You said Matthew has legal claim to the winery and the land ... so even if he leaves here, there'll be money. I'm only pointing out that you mustn't feel guilty about what he'll give up for you, Lauren,' she added defensively.

Lauren sighed. 'I know, Mother.' She patted Evelyn's hand reassuringly. 'It'll all work out. It's just that there's so much to tell him, all at once. I wish——' She caught her lower lip between her teeth and caught herself just in time. It would be so easy to throw her arms around her mother and tell her she was pregnant. But she wasn't a little girl any more. Besides, this wasn't a cut knee or a scratched cheek.

'Matt should be here soon,' she added. 'I mean, when he gets back to the Club and finds out that I fainted . . .'

'That worries me, Lauren. You be sure and see the doctor tomorrow.' Her mother smiled slightly and stroked Lauren's cheek. 'Are you sure you're all right now, child?'

'I'm fine,' she answered quickly. 'I told you, it was too much excitement and not enough food.'

'Yes, well, you've been through an awful lot for that man . . .' The doorbell's ring shattered Evelyn Webster's words.

'It's Matt,' Lauren whispered. Her hands fluttered to her cheeks. 'God, how will I tell him?'

The bell rang again and Evelyn got to her feet. 'Shall I tell him you're too sick to see him?'

Lauren shook her head. 'There's no point in delaying; I've got to get it over with.' She smoothed down her dress and gave her mother a reassuring smile. 'Would you mind going upstairs? I'd like to talk to him alone.'

She waited until her mother had vanished up the stairs. Then she ran her tongue along her lips and opened the front door.

'Sweetheart, are you all right?' Matt shouldered his way into the hall and grasped her by the shoulders. 'They told me you collapsed . . .'

'I'm fine,' she said quickly. 'I fainted, that was all. "Collapsed" sounds a lot more dramatic than it really was.'

'I heard that Dr Howell looked you over . . .'

'He did, and he said I'll live. Really, I'm okay.' She clasped Matt's hand in hers and led him into the small living room. 'Welcome to the Webster homestead,' she added with a faint smile.

'Why didn't you leave me a message?' he demanded, drawing her into his arms. 'I was frantic!'

'I guess I didn't think.' She laid her head against his chest again, listening to the steady thud of his heart. She should have listened to her mother, she thought suddenly. She should have let her tell Matt she was too ill to see him just yet, and given herself time to work out a plan. As it was, she had no idea of what to do first. She had so much to tell him, so much that he—that they—weren't prepared for. It was all tangled together like a Gordian knot. There had to be a place to start, but she hadn't the foggiest idea where that place was.

She sighed and closed her eyes, burrowing more closely into the warm comfort of his embrace. Whatever way she approached this, it was a mess worthy of Solomon.

'I have so much to tell you,' she said at last. 'I really don't know how to begin.'

'Lauren?'

'I have to tell you what happened after you left,' she said, moving away from him and sitting down on the couch. 'Matt, I . . . your father and I . . . we talked.'

He nodded his head. 'Yeah, I know. He told me.'

She looked up at him in surprise. 'Did he?'

He nodded again. 'He said . . . he said it wasn't as satisfactory a conversation as he'd have liked, but that he thought the two of you understood each other a little better now.'

She cocked her head to the side and stared at him. There was a rough, almost embarrassed edge to his voice. A faint surge of hope mushroomed within her. Had Arthur Chandler changed his mind? Had he decided to back off in the face of her determination?

'I . . . I don't understand,' she said cautiously. 'What did he tell you?'

Matt shrugged his shoulders. 'He explained what had happened between your mother and him years ago. About . . .' a faint line of colour rose to his cheeks, 'about this guy—Jim something or other.'

Lauren stared at him incredulously. 'He told you?'

He nodded and shoved his hands into his pockets. 'He wasn't going to, of course. But I didn't give him a hell of a lot of choice. I mean, the people at the next table couldn't wait to get hold of me and tell me that something had gone on between the two of you . . .'

She closed her eyes with relief and laid her head back against the couch.

'Thank God you know,' she sighed. 'I didn't know how to tell you what your father did to her. It was so cruel.'

'Come on, love. Let's not blow this out of proportion.'

Lauren's eyes blinked open. 'What did you say?'

Matt spread his hands and smiled sheepishly. 'Look, I know she's your mother, and I know that women tend to stick together, but . . .'

'What the hell does that have to do with it?' Lauren demanded, getting to her feet. 'There's such a thing as common decency!'

'Sure there is. But your mother knew what she was getting herself into, Lauren. She was of age, and this guy didn't make her any promises.'

'He said he loved her, Matt . . .'

'People say a lot of things, Lauren. That doesn't mean they have to pay for them for the rest of their lives.'

She opened her mouth and then closed it again. Her throat was so dry it ached, and she swallowed several times before she attempted to speak.

'You mean, only the woman has to pay . . .'

Matt shrugged his shoulders. 'I didn't say that. It's just that women tend to romanticise things—sometimes, what they call love is really just two people enjoying themselves. Women have to learn not to confuse a pleasant interlude with something more serious. They should learn to be more cautious.'

Every muscle in her body seemed to become rigid. 'More careful, you mean. Is that right?'

'That's one way of putting it, yes.' He smiled and opened his arms to her. 'Look, you and I don't have to fight about this. I think my father did the only thing he could, but I figured you might not agree. I know how close you and your mother are . . .'

Lauren shook her head and backed away from him. 'That hasn't got a thing to do with this, Matt.'

'Sure it has, Lauren. My father warned me you'd be defensive . . .'

'Is that what you think I am?' she asked, while part of her mind applauded the fact that she could still form a simple sentence.

'All right, call it what you like. Maybe you're just being loyal. The thing is, I really do understand how rough it must have been.'

'Do you?' she asked coldly.

He nodded. 'Of course. But try and see it from what's-his-name's viewpoint . . .'

'Jim,' she said evenly, and Matt nodded again.

'Right, Jim. He tried to explain things to her, but your mother wanted it her way.'

'What other way was there, for God's sake?'

'Remember what I told you, Lauren? You've got to take into account that there are always two sides to every story.'

He was still talking. She knew he was—she could see his mouth moving, the muscles in his face shifting, but his words were a low, blurred mélange of sounds. This couldn't be the man she'd fallen in love with, made love to, and yet . . . and yet . . .

'Tell me something,' she whispered. 'If that had been you . . .'

Matt's eyes searched hers. 'You mean, if I'd been in that kind of jam with a woman?' She nodded, afraid to trust her voice. He shrugged his shoulders. 'I've got to be honest, Lauren. I'd have felt as trapped as he did. No man likes to feel he's been . . . I don't know, forced into something. I don't think I'd have run—I know I wouldn't have let guilt snare me. Damn it, marriage is a big step. A man should propose because he wants to, not because he has to.'

The floor swayed beneath her feet, and she grasped the fireplace mantel for support. Matt moved towards her, and she shook her head.

'Get out,' she whispered. 'Please—get out, Matt.'

He was stunned. She could see it in his face, and somehow that hurt her more than anything he'd said. To know that he believed in the most chauvinistic kind of male philosophy about something that had changed her mother's entire life—that had, in fact, changed hers—drove a knife into her heart. And the secret of her own pregnancy twisted the hilt and drove the cold steel even deeper.

'Please,' she murmured, turning away and fighting against the tears that burned behind her eyelids, 'just go away.'

Matt's hands clamped on her arms and he spun her around to face him. 'Go away? What the hell are you talking about?'

'I don't know how much clearer I can make it,' she whispered. 'I want you to leave.'

'Come on, Lauren,' he growled. 'That's ridiculous! I knew you'd side with your mother——'

'Side with her?' she repeated. 'There aren't any sides in this kind of situation, Matt. There's right and there's wrong.'

'That's simplistic.'

'You mean moralistic, don't you?' She shook her head. 'Although I guess that's beyond your understanding.'

'Look, I refuse to fight over something like this. If you think your mother was right and my father was wrong, okay. Fine. So be it!'

'And Jim?' she whispered. 'Did he do the right thing or the wrong thing, Matt?'

He shrugged helplessly. 'What do you want me to say, Lauren? If it makes you feel better, I'll condemn him.'

'Don't patronise me,' Lauren snapped. 'A minute ago, he was your hero.'

'Dammit, Lauren—he was just a man in a tight spot. What did you expect him to do?'

She pulled free of Matt's arms and stared at him. Finally she took a deep breath. When she spoke, her voice was cold and steady.

'I have no expectations,' she said flatly. 'Not of him, and certainly not of you.' Her eyes met his. 'I don't want to see you any more, Matt.'

'Are you crazy? You want us to split up because I refuse to take your mother's side in something that happened a million years ago?'

'I told you, there aren't any sides. There's right and wrong, Matt. And we—you and I—are wrong. Wrong for each other.'

'What the hell are you talking about?' he growled, reaching out for her. His hands clamped on her arms. 'When are we wrong for each other, Lauren? When we work together? When we sail together?'

'I don't have to spell it out.'

'Maybe we're wrong for each other when we're in bed.' A surge of crimson flooded her face. 'Well?' he demanded. 'Tell me when we're wrong for each other, Lauren.'

'You're hurting me,' she said evenly. 'Please let go.'

He stared at her for a heartbeat longer and then his hands dropped to his sides.

'You haven't answered my question,' he said quietly.

She stepped back, automatically wrapping her arms around herself.

'If you could even doubt that what your father and . . . and that other man did was wrong . . .'

'Come on, Lauren . . .'

'If you could even question it . . .' She shook her head, and her hair flew wildly around her pale face. 'We really don't have anything more to say to each other, Matt.'

'I don't believe you, Lauren,' he grated, his voice tense with fury. 'From day one, all I've heard about is your mother. Your poor mother . . .'

'Get out of my house . . .'

'It's your mother's house, remember? She owns everything, including you.' Lauren turned her back, and Matt spun her around to face him. 'I was wrong when I said she controlled you: she owns you. She breathes for you, thinks for you . . .' His voice fell to a hoarse whisper. 'You're not really going to give up everything we have because I didn't take her side?' She lifted her chin defiantly. 'You want me to lie?' he asked softly. 'I'll tell you whatever you want to hear, Lauren.'

She felt a rushing current of tears dammed behind her eyelids.

'You can't,' she whispered brokenly, thinking of the life growing deep within her, knowing that it was the truth that would make his lie impossible to live with. 'It wouldn't work.'

His hands dropped to his sides and he nodded. 'It wouldn't, would it?' he murmured. 'Not as long as your mother owns you.' He ran his hands through his hair and then he turned away from her. Suddenly he stopped; she had to strain to hear his final, whispered words.

'The hell of it is, I'll always love you,' he said softly. 'I guess that makes me as crazy as you.'

A shiver raced through her. She watched as he opened the door; at the last second, he turned as if to speak. There was a sudden creak on the staircase behind her. A look of disgust transformed his face, then he yanked the door open and walked into the darkness.

'Lauren?' Her mother's footsteps clattered down the stairs as the door slammed shut. 'I couldn't help but overhear some of it. What arrogance!'

Lauren sagged against the door. The tears that had threatened began to spill down her cheeks.

'For God's sake, if you love him, don't worry about what he says about me. Don't put loyalty before opportunity.'

Her mother would never change, Lauren thought wearily. It would have been funny if it weren't so sad. Well, there was one sure way to put a stop to her mother's babbling. She drew in her breath in a long, wavering sigh.

'I'm pregnant,' she whispered.

Evelyn Webster's head snapped back. 'What?'

'Dr Howell's going to run some tests tomorrow just to confirm it, but I'm sure I am.'

Her mother's shriek was a wail of pain. 'How could you be so stupid?' she screamed. 'Is that why he left just now? Because you're pregnant?' Her face whitened. 'They never change, do they? But some things do, thank God. I'm not as stupid as I was twenty-two years ago, you know. There are blood tests, paternity suits . . .'

'He left because I sent him away,' Lauren said wearily. 'I didn't tell him I'm pregnant.'

'Will you please make sense?' her mother demanded. 'You have to tell him. Don't worry about his marrying you, Lauren. I told you, I'll see to that.'

'I have no intention of marrying Matt, Mother,' she said evenly.

Her mother inhaled sharply. 'You think an abortion is easier to live with? I doubt it, Lauren. And where would we get the money? We'd have to go to a clinic in San Francisco and probably stay at a hotel overnight.'

Minutes ago, as her world collapsed around her, Lauren would have sworn she had no idea of what to do next. The baby she carried was nothing but an abstraction; it seemed impossible to feel anything about it, one way or another. Now, suddenly, she knew precisely what she wanted. The knowledge filled her with a sense of purpose and determination.

'I'm going to have this baby,' she said calmly. 'I want it.'

Her comment stunned her mother into momentary silence.

'My God,' she whispered at last, 'haven't you learned anything from me?'

'I've learned it can be done.'

'I refuse to listen to another word of this nonsense. You cannot do this!'

'I can and I will,' Lauren said quietly. 'I can't stay here, of course . . .'

'You're damned right you can't.'

'. . . because I don't want Matt to know about it, but if I lived in San Francisco, you and I could still see each other often. I had several good job offers when I finished school, but I turned them down because you wanted me to come home, remember?'

Her mother laughed bitterly. 'And what a mistake that was!'

'Look, I'm going to do what I have to!'

'What you have to do is tell Matthew Chandler that you're carrying his child.'

Lauren grasped Evelyn's narrow shoulders in her hands. 'I'm not going to force Matt to marry me. Do you understand?'

Her mother pursed her lips. 'I think you're being very foolish. You——'

Lauren's voice was cold and without inflection. 'I warn you, Mother, if you ever say a word to him, you and I will be finished.'

'You don't mean that, Lauren!'

'I never meant anything more.'

The women's eyes caught and held. Evelyn Webster opened her mouth and then shut it. Finally, she shrugged her shoulders.

'It's your life, young woman,' she said sullenly. 'Have it your own way.'

In the dark, lifeless hour before dawn, it occurred to Lauren that the events of the evening had led, at least, to one positive thing. She had been graduated from 'child' to 'young woman'. Actually, she thought, as she buried her face in her pillow, 'fool' might be far more appropriate.

CHAPTER TWELVE

THE passage of time is like the ebb and flow of the ocean against the shore. Its caress is gentle, but each touch leaves a subtle change in its wake. And Matt had been touched by time; Lauren could see the faint spread of fine lines at the corners of his mouth and eyes as their gaze met across the fresh earth of her mother's grave.

'I only heard about your mother's death this morning,' he said. 'I wanted to pay my respects. I figured you'd be here.'

She pulled a handkerchief from her pocket and dried her eyes. 'Thanks,' she said quietly. 'That was kind of you.'

They stared at each other in uncomfortable silence. The wind had increased in intensity; dried leaves swirled in its grip, trapped momentarily in fierce, miniature whirlwinds.

'Lauren . . .'

'Matt . . .'

She laughed nervously as the words commingled. 'You first,' she said.

'I . . . I'm just amazed at how you look,' he said. 'I haven't seen you in three years, and you look just the same.'

She blushed and shook her head. 'That's not what my mirror says,' she murmured. 'But thanks anyway.'

Beside her, the minister cleared his throat. 'Ah, Miss Webster, if you're sure you can manage on your own, I have an appointment at noon . . .'

'I'm sorry, Reverend Dodd. Of course I can manage. Thank you again.'

She offered the minister her gloved hand, then watched as he walked down the hill. When finally his car pulled away and disappeared into the milky fog that had begun drifting in from the ocean, she looked at Matt and cleared her throat.

'Well, I guess . . . I guess it's time for me to go. My plane leaves in a couple of hours.'

'Yeah, sure,' Matt said quickly, 'The fog's getting heavy—it may take you a while to get to the airport.'

'I remember,' she said, smiling hesitantly. 'I haven't been away that long.'

'Three years is a long time, Lauren.'

His voice had a raw sound to it. She glanced at him and sighed when she saw the dark expression on his face. Of course, she thought, remembering the last time they'd seen each other. It must still be an unpleasant memory for him.

'Time passes quickly, doesn't it?' she asked in an artificially bright voice. 'Speaking of which,' she added, 'I really must get going.'

Matt nodded. 'I'll walk you to your car.'

They started down the gentle slope of the hill towards the parking lot. Long, opalescent fingers of fog caught them in a damp embrace. Lauren glanced at Matt as he walked silently beside her. If only she could tell him that the three years had seemed like an eternity, she thought suddenly. All she could remember of those endless days and months was the birth of her son—their son, the son Matt knew nothing about . . .

Stop it! she told herself fiercely, turning her face towards the distant sea barely visible through the fog. Why are you doing this to yourself? You have a new life and so does Matt. He has a wife ... A wife ...

'Careful!' he continued, grasping her elbow as she lost her footing momentarily on the damp grass.

'I'm okay,' she said calmly, but his touch had sent a shudder through her. She glanced at him from beneath half-lowered lashes, but he wasn't even looking at her. Oh God, she thought, please, please, don't let me feel anything. Don't let this happen. I don't love him any more, I don't, I don't ...

'I heard you'd moved East,' Matt said.

'Yes, yes, I did. New York.'

His tone was so polite, so formal. But then why wouldn't it be? It was her behaviour that made no sense. During the long flight west, it had been impossible not to speculate on the possibility of seeing him again. She'd told herself it wouldn't matter, one way or the other. The Matt and Lauren who filled her dreams were two other people. They belonged to the past, not the present. Their love affair was long over. All that was left were the long days and nights she'd spent missing him and aching for his touch. It was over, damn it, over, over, *over*.

'My mother told me you run the winery all by yourself now,' she said quickly.

He nodded. 'My father finally retired. Really retired, I mean,' he added with a faint smile. 'He bought a house on the beach at Santa Barbara. He's developed an obsession for golf. I think he's begun to relax and enjoy himself for the first time in his life. He's a changed man.'

Somehow, she managed a polite, impersonal smile.

'Well, of course the weather in Santa Barbara is

lovely,' she said, amazed at how much banal conversation you could manage when what you really wanted to do was burst into tears. Easy, she told herself, easy. The only reason you feel this shaky is because it's been a rough day. It has nothing to do with seeing Matt again. It has nothing to do with wishing you could turn back the clock and wipe out everything that happened after that long, wonderful afternoon in the wine shed . . .

'Here's my car,' she said, and she could hear the relief in her voice. She fumbled in her handbag for the key and then smiled brightly. 'Well, thanks for coming, Matt. It was very kind of you.' Without any warning, her voice trembled and broke, and, much to her horror, tears filled her eyes. 'I'm sorry,' she said quickly, 'I . . . I . . .'

'It's okay,' he said uncomfortably while she dabbed at her eyes. 'I know how hard a day this must have been for you.' She nodded her head, afraid to trust her voice. 'Look, maybe you'd like a cup of coffee or some lunch . . . We could stop in San Jacinto.'

For a timeless moment, her pulse quickened. Was it possible? Did he really want to prolong their time together? Her eyes met his and the hope that had flared within her died. His brows were drawn together in a scowl. God, she thought, how could she have been so foolish? He was probably counting the minutes until he could get away. After all, here she was, the only mourner at the funeral, and here he was, stuck with her out in the middle of nowhere, and all because he'd been polite.

She stuffed her handkerchief into her pocket and shook her head.

'Thanks for the offer, but I'm fine. Really. And I

have a plane to catch.'

'Sure, I understand. You probably can't wait to get home.'

She thought of her son—their son—the beautiful child Matt knew nothing about, the only thing that made her lonely life bearable, and she took a deep breath.

'Yes,' she murmured, 'that's right.'

'Yeah,' he said gruffly, 'well, I guess that's it, then. I . . . Lauren, I . . .'

He looked so uncomfortable that she wanted to touch his hand and tell him she understood, but instead she smiled and opened the door to the car. She slid behind the wheel and stuck the key into the ignition. The engine whined weakly and then died. No, she thought—no, please, it has to start, it has to!

'Damn,' she muttered.

'Try it again,' suggested Matt. 'Maybe it's cold.'

She caught her lip between her teeth and did as he suggested. This time, there was no sound at all.

'Now what?' She slapped her gloved hand lightly against the wheel. I have to get away from here, she thought. I must. 'Not a telephone in miles,' she said aloud. 'And I've got to get to the airport.'

'Let me take a look under the bonnet. Maybe it's something simple—a loose wire or something.'

She yanked on the release and watched as Matt raised the hood and peered under it. After a few minutes, he slammed it closed and shook his head.

'I don't see anything. Did you rent it in San Francisco?' She nodded. 'Well, tell them to come out and take care of it. I'll drive you to a phone in San Jacinto.'

Lauren glanced over at his small, sleek Ferrari. The thought of sitting in such close quarters with him made her ache, but there was little choice. She nodded and stepped from the rental car. As he helped her into the Ferrari, his touch was polite and impersonal—but then what else would it be? she thought, settling into the leather seat beside him. Just because she was falling apart, why should he? He was happy, after all. She knew he was; her mother had made a point of telling her so. He had the Chandler Winery all to himself now, and he had a wife, a beautiful, wealthy young woman from Los Angeles or San Francisco or some damned place like that. Well, she was happy, too, she reminded herself. She had a terrific job and a handsome apartment and her son.

Lauren caught her bottom lip between her teeth and stared blindly at the barely visible road ahead. Matt was driving with easy confidence, even though they seemed to be travelling through a milky cloud. She shivered and he glanced over at her.

'Are you cold?'

She shook her head. 'I'm okay,' she said quickly.

Liar, she thought, liar, liar, liar. She wasn't okay. She hadn't been okay since the night she'd sent him out of her life. Oh, sure, she could kid herself into thinking everything was fine. Lately, there had even been entire days when she didn't think of him and wonder what he was doing and how he looked and . . .

But you couldn't lie to yourself in the cold, cruel hours before dawn, she thought, leaning her head back against the cool leather seat. How many times had she woken with Matt's name on her lips? In the pale grey light of the city's awakening, how many times had she taken her son into her arms and cried for all the moments and days and years he'd never share with the man who was his father? Sometimes, she thought that denying father and son to each other was a cruelty that outweighed her own need for self-protection; once, only once, she had weakened and almost contacted Matt to tell him about their child. But she hadn't, thank God, she hadn't . . . and it was a damned good thing, too, because it was just about then her mother had told her Matt was married.

'Aren't you seeing that Vice-President any more?' her mother had asked during one of her visits East. 'He seemed like such a nice man.'

Lauren had explained that yes, her boss was nice and no, she wasn't dating him any more because she had sensed that he was getting serious about her and she didn't feel that way about him, she didn't feel that way about anyone, and that was when her mother had told her about Matt, told her that she might as well put him out of her mind for ever. And she had, hadn't she? Of course she had.

Oh, God, who was she kidding? She loved him! She loved him as much now as she ever had. No, she thought with a sudden, sharp insight, no, she loved him even more, as if by doing so she could make up for the years they'd lost. If only the strength of his love had matched hers. If only you could slow the sands of time from running through the glass. But it was too late, too late. Everything they had shared and been and done together belonged to the past. All she had were memories. That was all she would ever have. And whatever life she thought she'd created for herself during these past three years was meaningless.

'Lauren? Are you all right?'

Her head sprang up and she stared at Matt. 'I'm sorry,' she mumbled. 'I . . . I was daydreaming. Did you say something?'

He was intent on the road ahead. 'I asked you if you were okay. You were so quiet.'

'I was just thinking about that darned car,' she said brightly. 'You'd think they'd check them out before renting them to people, wouldn't you?'

Matt nodded. 'Yeah, well, I'll stop at the first phone booth in town. Unless . . . unless you'd like me to take you to the airport?'

'Oh no,' she said quickly. She took a deep breath and forced a smile to her face. 'I mean, there's no need to do that. Let the rental people worry about getting me to my plane on time. They can send a car for me or pay for a cab.'

Matt glanced over at her and smiled. 'That sounds like executive talk!'

She laughed softly. 'Did it? Well, I'm not in the secretarial pool any more, you know.'

'So I heard. I . . . I bumped into your mother a while back. She told me you were working for a hotel in New York.'

'She never mentioned it.'

Matt shrugged his shoulders. 'Well, it wasn't the most cordial of meetings,' he said wryly.

Lauren sighed. 'Yes, I can imagine.'

'Which hotel? I go East on business sometimes.'

'A group of them,' she said quickly. 'Actually, I'm with their convention department. It's an interesting job.'

'I'm sure it is,' he said politely.

'And you're running things at Chandler's. I saw an ad for your estate-bottled wines in the *New York Times* last week. I guess they've been successful, hmm?'

'Yes, they've done well.'

The fog had thickened outside the car. It muffled the sounds of the road, emphasising the silence that settled between them. Lauren peered out of the window. The trip was taking so much longer than it would have if the weather had been good. Where were they? she wondered. The road had narrowed— yes, they'd just turned off the highway and on to the back road leading into San Jacinto. That meant they had at least another ten minutes together. She looked at Matt and then down at her lap.

'I passed the winery on the way to the cemetery this morning,' she said, tossing words, any words, into the heavy silence. 'It looked the same as always.'

'So do you,' he said, glancing at her and then back at the road.

'You said that before.'

'It's the truth, Lauren. You look as beautiful as I remember.'

The words themselves stunned her as much as the way in which he'd said them. His voice had a husky softness to it, as if he were making love to her.

'I like your hair that way,' he told her. 'But I liked it better when you wore it loose and soft around your face.'

He reached across and touched his fingers to her hair. The touch of his hand was like a flame searing her skin.

'Don't!' she exclaimed sharply, pulling away from him. 'Don't do that, Matt!'

'God, I'm sorry, Lauren, I . . .'

'It's all right,' she whispered, huddling against the door.

'No, no, it's not,' he said quickly, his eyes riveted on the road ahead. 'I don't know what the hell got into me. I——'

She put her gloved hand to her lips but a muffled sob escaped her.

'Lauren, love—please, I didn't mean to upset you. I'm sorry. I . . .'

She shook her head, not daring to look at him, praying he'd think she was reacting to her mother's death. He had no way of knowing she'd done all her crying when the hospital called and told her about her mother's accident and subsequent coma. She leaned her forehead against the window, praying for the drive to end.

He repeated her name, and suddenly the car swerved to the side of the road and bounced along the shoulder, the brakes squealing as he brought it to a stop.

'Lauren,' Matt said again, the word a whispered plea, and with a cry she turned towards him. His face was filled with pain and need, and a sweet, sharp surge of triumph shot through her as she realised that he still loved her, and then there was no more time to think because she was in his arms.

Her mouth sought his and they clung together like the survivors of a catastrophe, each seeking the other's warmth and reassurance. There was the warm, salty taste of tears on her tongue. Were they hers? Were they his? It didn't matter. Nothing mattered but the joy of being in Matt's arms. The long, lonely years of separation were swept aside like thistle seeds in a gale. There was no past, no present. There was only this single, suspended moment, this warp in the fabric of the universe in which love could shelter.

'I love you,' Matt whispered, his lips warm against hers. 'I've always loved you, Lauren. Always.'

She trembled at his whispered admission. His

mouth and hands had told her the same thing, but hearing him say it filled her with a greater happiness than she'd ever known.

'Yes,' she sighed, 'yes, I love you, too, Matt. I never stopped.'

And then, as if from a distance, Lauren heard her own words. What were they doing to each other, except reminding themselves of what they could never have? There was no going back. Time was a straight, infinite line, not a circle with no beginning and no end. You could recapture the past for a moment, but that was all. What had flared to life a moment ago was as fragile as the flame of a match lit against the dark. With a muted cry, she tore her lips from his and buried her face against his shoulder.

'Matt, we can't! We mustn't do this.'

He put his hand under her chin and tilted her face up to his. 'What happened to us, Lauren?' he demanded in a husky whisper. 'We loved each other so much.'

'It doesn't matter any more,' she sighed. 'It's too late.'

His arms tightened around her. 'Listen to me,' he said urgently. 'I have to tell you ... I've thought about it over and over. I was such a fool, Lauren. I should have kept my stupid mouth shut that night.'

'Matt . . .'

'I was going to ask you to marry me. Instead, I ended up losing you.'

The knowledge, even though it came years too late, thrilled her. 'You were going to ask me to marry you?' she whispered.

'Of course I was. It was going to be the most wonderful night of my life, and instead—instead, I lost everything.'

'You didn't lose everything.'

'Everything,' he repeated, his voice hoarse. 'And it was all because I couldn't understand how much your mother meant to you.'

Her eyes met his. 'Nobody ever meant more to me than you did,' she said before she could stop herself.

'That night . . .' He drew back and cupped her face in his hands. 'I was wrong, Lauren.'

'Matt, it doesn't matter. It's too late . . .'

'Dammit,' he said in a fierce whisper, 'it's not too late for me to tell you the truth. It's been driving me crazy all these years. I don't know why I didn't see it your way from the start.'

She shook her head, unwilling to remember how callously he'd treated the story of her mother's betrayal by the man she had loved. It would only remind her once again of why she had never told him of her own pregnancy and of their child.

'Don't,' she murmured. 'What's done is done.'

'But my father was wrong, Lauren. He shouldn't have promoted a man who'd been using your mother that way.'

His words seemed to echo through the confined space. 'What did you say?' she whispered finally.

'I don't want to fight about it again, Lauren,' he said quickly. 'You were right; I was insensitive.'

She shook her head impatiently. 'Matt, please. Exactly what did your father tell you that night?'

He took a deep breath. 'I told you!'

'No, you didn't tell me anything, remember? You simply said your father had told you what had happened between our parents, and I assumed it was the same story he'd told me. Please, Matt, what did he say?'

'Lauren, what's the point? Okay, okay. He told me

your mother came to see him years before and told him some story about a guy who worked at the winery—Jim something or other, I think. He was about to be promoted, and your mother told my father that she'd been dating this man—well, sleeping with him, actually ... Lauren, why go through this again?' Matt said unhappily. 'Isn't it bad enough that we fought over it once?'

'You've got to tell me the rest,' she said in a low, urgent voice. 'Please!'

He smiled faintly. 'I can't deny you anything, my love,' he said softly, brushing the hair back from her cheeks. 'although I don't know what good it can do to go over it again. Your mother told my father this guy had broken off with her. She wanted my father to deny the man the promotion—he was going to head up Personnel and she said she wanted to make sure he wouldn't have the chance to seduce other naïve young women. My old man thought that she was just being vindictive.'

'Oh, Matt!'

Lauren's cry trembled between them, and then she began to sob. He drew her closer to him, his hands stroking and soothing her, his lips moving softly across her face.

'I knew it would upset you,' he said roughly. 'Why did you insist on hearing the whole damn thing again?'

'Because I never heard it the first time, Matt,' she said in a choked whisper. 'You see, that's not what really happened.'

'What are you saying, Lauren?'

'I mean, it wasn't like at all. But your father counted on my silence. He was so sure he had me cornered that he felt safe telling you any story he

wanted to. He never dreamed I'd tell you the truth.'
Lauren took a deep breath. The truth would change
nothing, she knew, but at least it would erase some of
the hurt they'd inflicted upon each other.

'Your father arranged things so you had to leave
the Club that night,' she said quietly. 'He did it so he
could tell me he wanted me out of your life. When I
refused, he ... he told me about my mother—and
about myself, too. He told me I was born out of
wedlock—my father was that man.'

'Jim?' asked Matt. Lauren nodded. 'Then—that
whole story about a promotion . . .'

'It was all a lie. Jim knew my mother was
pregnant, and he ran away and deserted her. Your
father arranged it, because Jim wasn't his employee.
He was his godson.'

Slowly, her eyes never leaving his, Lauren told him
the entire story, ending with Arthur Chandler's
threat to expose the old scandal to the town.

When she'd finished, Matt shook his head.

'I can't believe it,' he muttered hoarsely. 'That's
blackmail!'

She nodded in agreement. 'That's what I said. I
said I'd tell you what he'd threatened—and he said I
could, of course, but if I did, you'd walk out on him.'

'Goddamned right I would have,' he muttered, his
voice hoarse with anger.

'And he said that leaving Chandler's would kill
you. But I ... I counted on the fact that our love
could overcome everything,' she said, her voice
dropping to a whisper. She bent her head and leaned
her forehead against his chin. 'I believed that until
... until ...'

'Until I came through the door yapping about how
your mother had an exaggerated view of things,' said

Matt with a groan. 'And you—God, you had no way of knowing that I didn't know the truth.' He shuddered and his arms closed tightly around her. 'You must have hated my guts!'

'Never,' she said quickly. 'I never hated you—I was hurt and angry and upset because——' Her words tumbled to a halt. She had almost told him about the baby. In the mad rush to correct their terrible misunderstanding, she'd forgotten completely that he was married. Suddenly, that fact loomed up before her like a brick wall.

'Because of what?' he prompted.

Lauren drew a deep, shuddering breath. 'This is all water over the dam,' she said, moving out of his embrace. 'I'm glad we straightened things out, but . . .' Her voice broke, and she fought for control. 'There's nothing we can do to change what's happened, Matt. Not without . . . without hurting others and . . . and . . .' She pressed her gloved hand to her mouth and shook her head. 'I think you'd better take me into town,' she whispered.

He stared at her in silence, his eyes searching hers, then he turned away and exhaled sharply.

'Yes, of course,' he muttered, turning on the engine. 'Forgive me, Lauren. I shouldn't have . . . I don't have the right anymore.'

She couldn't trust herself to answer. Neither of them had the right, she reminded herself. But the brief moment of indiscretion had been worth everything. She knew now that Matt's love for her had been as strong and true as hers for him.

She risked a glance at him as the Ferrari turned on to Main Street. Her son looked just like his father, she thought with pride. In less than six hours, she'd be back in New York, back with the perfect little boy she'd left with her housekeeper. She would never tell Matt about him—that would only add to his pain—but knowing that he would have wanted their child, just as he had wanted her, filled her with bittersweet joy. At least she had her son, she thought, even thought she knew in her heart that not even he could fill the emptiness that would always be part of her life.

The car swerved to the kerb and stopped next to the San Jacinto Diner. There was a telephone booth just outside. Lauren grasped the door handle and forced a smile to her lips.

'Thanks for everything, Matt,' she said softly. Don't cry, she told herself fiercely. You mustn't cry.

He nodded his head and cleared his throat. 'Do you have change for the phone?'

'Change?' she repeated blankly.

'So you can call about your car.'

'The car—yes, of course.' She smiled and shook her head. 'I—er—I don't know. Let me see . . .'

She opened her handbag and rummaged through it. 'My wallet's in here somewhere,' she murmured, stripping off her gloves and tossing them into her lap. 'I know it is.' She heard his sudden, sharp gasp and she looked up. 'Matt? What is it?'

His voice was hoarse. 'Why aren't you wearing your wedding ring?'

Her eyes lifted to his and then she frowned and looked down at her left hand.

'Wedding ring?' she repeated in a puzzled tone. 'But I'm not married. I never . . .'

'But your mother . . . Lauren, she told me you'd married.'

She frowned and shook her head. 'She couldn't have. It isn't true. I never . . .'

'Lauren—God, would I make a mistake about something like that? I stormed over to see her last winter—I'd confronted her before, demanding to know where you'd gone, but she'd insisted you didn't want to see me. This last time, I told her I wanted to hear that from you, not from her. I told her I was going to get you back—I said I'd move heaven and earth to do it, if I had to, and she . . . she said you were married, that you were happy.'

'Last winter?' she repeated softly. 'But that was when . . .' Her words drifted into silence. That was when she'd told her mother her boss had got too serious about their relationship. That was when her mother had told her Matt had taken a wife. Anger flared within her. Was there no end to her mother's interference? Hadn't she ever stopped? Even after everything that had happened . . .

A sudden, desperate hope surged through her. Please, she thought, please, Mother, let me find out that you were predictable, right to the last. For the first time in her life, Lauren prayed that Evelyn Webster had gone right on trying to arrange her life for her. She cleared her throat and focused her eyes on Matt's. There was only one question left to ask, and it took all the courage she possessed to ask it.

'Matt?' Her voice was faint and hoarse. 'How . . . how's your wife?'

A bewildered look swept across his face. 'My wife? Lauren, love, I'm not married. How could you have even thought I'd ever . . .'

She laughed aloud and flung herself into his arms. 'Oh, Matt,' she whispered, 'Matt, I love you, I love you, *I love you*!'

His arms closed around her. 'I don't understand one bit of what just happened,' he said warily, 'but I have the damnedest feeling your mother's part of it.'

Lauren laughed again. 'I can't believe it! She couldn't resist one last bit of tampering—she wanted to make sure we wouldn't try to find each other and that I wouldn't pass up a chance to marry.'

'Let me get this straight,' he said carefully. 'You thought I was married?' She nodded her head. 'And I thought you . . .' His arms tightened around her. 'Oh, my love, I'm afraid to let myself believe this is real. I'm afraid I'll wake up and find that you're not really in my arms—that you're a dream, that this dream is just more real than all the others that have filled my nights since you left.'

Lauren lifted her face to his and kissed his mouth tenderly. 'I'm not a dream, my darling,' she said.

A smile touched the corners of his mouth. 'Convince me.'

She laughed softly and drew his head down to hers. After a long, sweet moment, Matt drew back and grinned. 'That's better,' he murmured. 'But I'm still not certain. Have you got any other evidence to offer?'

'Absolutely,' she whispered shamelessly. 'But it will have to wait. Otherwise I'm going to miss my flight to New York.'

'You're not getting away from me again, Lauren Webster. I'm the fool who lost you once. You don't think I'm going to let that happen again, do you?'

She smiled at him. 'Not if I have anything to say about it. But I still have to go back to New York. I . . . I left something important behind.'

'More important than this?' he murmured, kissing her slowly and deliberately. 'I want to lock you away somewhere for the next few days and make love to you.'

'That's wonderful,' she sighed.

'And then I'll just let you out long enough to marry you.'

'That's even better. But I still have to go to New York first.'

'Lord, you are one hell of a determined woman!' Matt laughed with mock indignation. 'Okay, you win. New York first. We'll go together, although I can't imagine what could be that important!'

Lauren took a deep breath. There was so much to tell him, she thought, so much to share . . .

'Do you like children?' she asked softly.

He grinned. 'I love 'em. Is this an offer? Because if it is, I might as well put my order in now. I want a houseful of near-sighted, tow-headed little girls who look just like their mother!'

'How do you feel about dark-haired little boys who look like their daddy?'

'I'll want some of those, too,' Matt said solemnly. 'Definitely.'

'Oh, I'm so glad to hear that, my love, because I've already started filling your order. That's why I have to go to New York.' Lauren smiled happily. 'You see, I left your son there. His name is Matthew Webster Chandler, he's almost three years old, he's about thirty-six inches tall and he has his father's blue eyes and his dark hair and he's just crazy about sailboats in the bath tub.!'

It was amazing, Lauren thought as Matt's mouth found hers, but his tears tasted as sweet as honey.

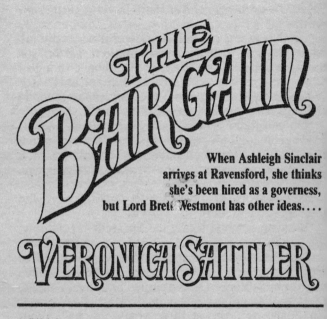

Harlequin Presents

Coming Next Month

1031 WINTER SUNLIGHT Susan Alexander
Sophie can't believe it. Max is offering her what she most wants. But marriage with Max, an eminent Austrian baron, is not for her. She can love him, have an affair with him. But not marriage!

1032 NIGHT OF THE CONDOR Sara Craven
Crossing the world to join her fiancé in Peru changes spoiled wealthy Leigh Frazier's life. For in meeting the fascinating archeologist Dr. Rourke Martinez, she is drawn under the spell of the high Andes, in a new and dangerous embrace....

1033 THE ONE THAT GOT AWAY Emma Darcy
Substituting as skipper on her father's fishing boat, chartered by American football player and movie star, Taylor Marshall, Jillian realizes after she falls in love, that to him it's just another game. And will she be just another trophy?

1034 SINGLE COMBAT Sandra Field
Lydia grew up without love. She's learned to live without it, she thinks. Now here's James who simply refuses to be put off like the other men who had proposed marriage. If she could only let herself trust him....

1035 IF LOVE BE BLIND Emma Goldrick
Penn Wilderman, suffering from temporary snow blindness, is convinced by her manner that Philomena Peabody, who's looking after him, is a sweet little old lady. This doesn't worry Phil, until in order to win a custody battle for his son, Penn asks Phil to marry him!

1036 DON'T ASK FOR TOMORROW Susanne McCarthy
Kate hires skipper Sean McGregor to help prove that her late husband had discovered the wreck, the _Belle Etoile_. Sean had worked with her husband, and guards a secret concerning him. But Kate soon discovers that she must give up the past—or betray her love.

1037 TANGLED HEARTS Carole Mortimer
Love, hate, loyalty all mix in Sarah's mind. She wants to run. But no matter what it costs, she can't let anyone else in her family be denied love because of Garrett Kingham—and her fear of facing him again.

1038 ELDORADO Yvonne Whittal
Gina's schoolgirl crush on Jarvis had long been replaced by a more mature emotion. She is woman enough now to know that her feelings are somehow being manipulated. And she can't help wondering if Jarvis is really interested in her—or just in her property.

Available in December wherever paperback books are sold, or through Harlequin Reader Service:

In the U.S.
901 Fuhrmann Blvd.
P.O. Box 1397
Buffalo, N.Y. 14240-1397

In Canada
P.O. Box 603
Fort Erie, Ontario
L2A 5X3

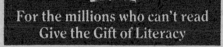

**For the millions who can't read
Give the Gift of Literacy**

**One out of five adults in North America
cannot read or write well enough
to fill out a job application
or understand the directions on a bottle of medicine.**

**You can change all this by joining the fight
against illiteracy.**

For more information write to:
Contact, Box 81826, Lincoln, Neb. 68501
In the United States, call toll free: 1-800-228-8813

**The only degree you need
is a degree of caring**

Six exciting series
for you every month...
from Harlequin

Harlequin Romance·
The series that started it all

Tender, captivating and heartwarming...
love stories that sweep you off to faraway places
and delight you with the magic of love.

Harlequin Presents·
Powerful contemporary love
stories...as individual as the
women who read them

The No. 1 romance series...
exciting love stories for you, the woman of today...
a rare blend of passion and dramatic realism.

Harlequin Superromance®
It's more than romance...
it's Harlequin Superromance

A sophisticated, contemporary romance-fiction
series, providing you with a longer,
more involving read...a richer mix of complex plots,
realism and adventure.